Magic in the Moonlight

Dria Andersen

To my husband, who was my sounding board, my cheerleader, my critique partner, and all the things I needed to finish this project. I appreciate every hour, every word of input, and most of all, your unwavering support.

To my family, who had to deal with mommy being on in another world for hours at a time. Thank you for your patience.

To my aunt Cathy who gave me my first love of romance stories, I thank you for allowing me to raid your bookshelf.

Thank you to every fan who continues to stick with me while telling the stories playing in my head. I appreciate each and every one of you.

Also, I would like to give a special thanks to Pikko House for the feedback and help I get from your alpha readers.

Author's Note

This is book two of the Georgia Arcana series and I'm very excited. I wanted to do something a little different with the lead male MC. Israel is very rough around the edges. I don't think he cares that he's a bad person. I know that will be a little off-putting to some readers, but he's working on himself, if only for Audrey and I think that's beautiful. This is my first time trying to write a second chance romance, and y'all already know I'm not one for angst, so while, they have their issues, there's not a lot of turmoil. I likes easy romance and this story is no different.

There are a couple of trigger warnings for death and grief. Well...and language if that kind of thing bothers you. I hope you guys like these two and enjoy the ride of their relationship.

Chapter One

There were precisely two sounds in Israel Black's office. The drumming of his fingers as he awaited an answer to a question that needed no posing...and the whimpering that was already getting on his nerves. The two shifters in front of him traded looks before sneaking another glance to the corner of his massive office.

Another whine.

Israel narrowed his eyes on the owner of that whimpering, a look that shut the noise down with the quickness—satisfied that he could receive his answer with no further distractions— he gave his undivided attention to the two males in front of him. Though powerful, the two lion shifters in front of him were merely low-level enforcers, fodder, really, which is why they'd been sent to get the answers to his most pressing question.

Where the hell was his wife?

Israel stopped the drumming and waited...

The first shifter cleared his throat. "We found her, sir."

Satisfaction filled him, but none of it showed on his face. "Then why is she not here with me?"

The two shifters —who he and Eli had dubbed 'the twins' since they started working with him at the same time—shared a look between them, the nervous glance his first hint that he was going to be pissed. They once again looked towards the corner.

"She's protected," came their answer.

Fury rose at the thought. Who would dare take something of his? "By who?"

How he managed to sound calm was anyone's guess.

"The Taylor pack."

A tick in his jaw was his only reaction. But the men who had worked for him for a while understood what it meant. They took a slow step back with another glance at the last person he'd sent looking for his wife. That male was currently stuck in his leopard form, leashed and muzzled. It was a great reminder of Israel's views on failure. Another whimper sounded, and Israel lifted his hand and twisted. But, he soon realized that the choking sounds were no better than the whining. He released his hold on the leopard's airway and went back to drumming his fingers against the desk.

He needed to think about this latest development. On the one hand, his wife was protected from his enemies. On the other hand, her retrieval became that much trickier. He knew the Taylor pack. She would be protected on their territory. No one left Taylor land alive unless under their express permission. For now, he could use that to his advantage.

Israel had a hundred things that needed attending to on his desk. A few dozen enemies to sort through to figure out who was striking at him, and yet, he was getting ready to chase down his errant wife. It was annoying, to say the least. From the moment he'd laid eyes on Audrey, an impulsiveness he was not known for had gripped him. Her power had called to him, and the woman herself was a siren he couldn't look away from. Their whirlwind weekend, up to and including their impulsive marriage, had been out of character for him. When he saw something he wanted, he took it and then discarded it when done. With her, he had a ferocious need to own her, possess her. It kept him up for long nights before he finally approached her.

He thought things had been going well with them, but then she'd run off. He didn't know why, but she had promised herself to him, and he would make her keep that promise. No matter how rash it had been.

He had no intention of allowing her defiance any longer.

He pressed the button for his secretary. "Have my plane ready." He instructed when she answered. He turned his attention to the twins. "Set up a meeting with Jeremiah Taylor. He's their current alpha, yes?"

They nodded.

"We land in Georgia in two hours. I want that meeting when I land."

They scrambled from the office to do his bidding. Israel gathered his suit jacket and walked out, his primary enforcer flanking him the moment he entered the executive elevator.

"Jet should be ready by the time we arrive, Lucky," Eli informed him.

Israel grunted, having no doubt. He paid people amply to be where he told them to be. He got into the sleek town car idling right at the elevator, Eli entering the back seat behind him. Israel tapped his fingers on his thigh, his only outward sign of aggravation.

"You sure this can't wait, boss?"

He turned his head to his head enforcer. "So long as my wife is out from under my protection, she's a liability and thus a threat to us."

Eli nodded. "We should have no problems landing in that territory. JT took out Jedidiah."

Once again, Israel found himself impressed by the wolf. He'd had dealings with the Taylors before and had never had any doubt about their power or ruthlessness. To take out a powerful rootworker like Jedidiah, though. That was a feat. It seemed the young Taylor had learned a lot from his father. He looked forward to seeing him again.

"How many enforcers you think we can get away with on Taylor territory?" Israel asked.

Eli sighed. "The Taylors don't even play the radio. We'll be lucky if we can get the twins in with us into town without starting anything."

Israel wiped a hand down his face in aggravation. He only had to deal with the wolves for as long as it took to get his wife back.

Chapter Two

Lunch in a bar had never been something Audrey Marks had envisioned for herself. In fact, it was the exact opposite. She'd been dragging her mama out of bars since she was old enough to ride a bicycle and had promised her ten-year-old self that she'd never drink, never mind voluntarily step foot into a bar.

And yet...

Here she sat, tearing up a plate of the best chicken wings she'd ever had, talking shit with her favorite cousins. Lore was a hole-in-the-wall bar, home to the Taylor's motorcycle gang. The place was clean, full of fine men, and a place where Audrey was comfortable. She, Nic, and Ness sat eating at a table tucked behind the pool tables. There had been so many changes to her life since Grandmother had died, and of all of them, being able to sit with her cousins in the middle of the day was one of her favorites.

"So, you've been doing okay at the brewery?" Ness asked, snapping her fingers in front of Audrey's face.

She sucked her teeth and used her forearm to push her hair out of her face. "Girl, I'm paying attention to you." Audrey rolled her eyes.

"And it's going well. Me and Dame got plans to expand into other beverages by next year."

"Long-term plans. I like it," Nic said, bumping her shoulder with Audrey's.

Long-term plans...yeah. So long as Audrey kept one step ahead of a certain somebody, she should have no problem staying in Georgia for the long term. She shuddered as memories from last night's dream filled her thoughts. They were getting stronger, more vivid. Soon enough, she was almost certain he'd be able to use them to find her. She wished she knew how much time she had. So far, the spells she'd been trying kept him out of her thoughts, but her dreams...

That was a whole other matter.

Audrey wiped her hands off and tucked the short red strands of her hair behind her ear. The color was different than yesterday and the day before that. The quick spells were a great way to stay ahead of her 'problem,' and they helped her practice her spellwork.

She pushed the plate away from her. She was full, and thinking about her situation-ship had butterflies in her stomach. Nicole smiled and looked behind Audrey; she didn't even have to turn around and find out why. JT's energy heated her back, his wolf aggressive and dominant. The shifter was a good match for her cousin. He plopped refills for their drinks down on the table and leaned over, and kissed his mate. Nicole eagerly returned his greeting, and Ness pretended to gag across the table. Audrey snickered.

"You sound like a whole hater, Ness," JT teased, kissing the top of her head before doing the same to Audrey. "Why you ain't tell me Ms. Dawn was in town?"

Ness turned her panicked face towards the entrance of the bar. "My mama's not in town."

JT frowned. "I literally just saw her when I dropped some stuff off to Ms. Shelby."

"Just now?" Audrey said, sharing a startled look with Ness.

Ness whipped out her cellphone and called her mother. She put it on speaker and bit her lip as it rang. Her leg was bouncing as they listened to the rings. Ness ran a hand over her cornrows and fiddled with the big hoop earrings she wore. Her cousin's beautiful face was scrunched in worry. She furrowed her neatly trimmed eyebrows, her teeth worrying her full bottom lip.

Audrey put a hand on her cousin's leg, sending her calming energy. "I'm sure it's nothing serious, Ness."

"I just...this place triggers her, ya' know."

"She looked fine when I saw her," JT assured her.

"Hey, baby!" Aunt Dawn answered in a chipper voice.

Ness's shoulders drooped in relief. "Mama, where you at?"

"Well, I'm doing fine, and yourself?"

Audrey hid her smile. Her aunt's chastisement was said in the same happy voice.

"Mama."

"Vanessa, I'm a grown ass woman. I don't answer to you." Aunt Dawn said sweetly.

Audrey's heart rate accelerated when she heard the voices in the background.

"Ah hell no," Nic whispered.

"We're over at Kit's if you must know," Dawn finally answered.

Oh God! "At my mama's house? In Denver?" *Please be in Denver*, Audrey prayed, knowing it was a futile prayer.

"Hey, niece!" Dawn greeted her.

"Is that my baby?" Katherine, Kit, Marks called from the background.

Audrey's heart dropped to her stomach, and she dropped her head onto the table.

"We finna cook. Y'all should come by when you're done with work," Kit said into the phone.

"Who all over there?" Nic asked, her eyes wide.

"You'll find out when you get here." Was Dawn's answer.

Ness stabbed the end call button on her phone and cursed. "They couldn't even act right for the funeral. No way they're all together. Right?"

"Shit." Audrey wiped her hands and stood. "We need to find out."

The three of them rushed from the bar and loaded into Nic's SUV. It took a mere five minutes to pull up to the old house that Audrey had not seen the inside of for years. She'd barely worked up the courage to walk around the outside a couple of weeks ago. She hadn't been inside since they'd left Georgia, after her father died. There were two cars in the yard where there had been none just two days ago.

It wasn't the only thing that changed. The windows were opened, the porch cleaned off, and someone had already started weeding in the front. How long had her mother and aunt been here? Instead of getting out, the three cousins sat in the running car; she was sure each debating an escape plan.

Nic cursed in the driver's seat as Aunt Lauren came out onto the porch and waved. "All them prayers, and yet I still ended up in hell."

Audrey snickered. "Not too much on my Auntie. Cut the car off, and let's get this over with."

Ness sighed loudly and opened the backdoor. "My mama ain't staying with us. I'm not finna deal with it."

"We should make them stay here together. That's a surefire way to run them off without either of us having to lift a finger," Nic murmured.

"You so damn mean," Audrey laughed, getting out of the passenger side.

By the time they reached the porch, all four of the Fouche sisters were waiting for them. The women were beautiful, each of them carrying those cat-like eyes known to the Fouche women. They were varying shades of brown and dressed in wildly differing styles, from her Aunt Lauren's chic jumpsuit to her Aunt Shelby's casual jeans and sweat shirt. Audrey eyed her Aunt Dawn, Ness' mother, smiling at the woman's baggy overalls. It looked like she'd started up painting again. That was a good sign.

"How'd you escape husband number five, or did you drag him

with you?" Nic was the first to break the silence, taking a dig at her mother.

Aunt Lauren cut a look to her sisters. "See how she talks to me? I don't know what I did to deserve—"

"—I can think of at least a dozen things that made you eligible for that karma." Kit cut her sister off.

Her aunts all cackled, ignoring the death glare Aunt Lauren sent them.

"What is going on here," Audrey asked before the sisters descended into arguing.

Her eyes roamed her mother's face, looking for tell-tale signs that she'd started drinking again. Relief filled her at her mother's sharp, clear gaze. Kit's face had filled out, and she looked relaxed...happy even. Audrey had gotten her high cheekbones from her mother, same as her small nose and full lips. She was the spitting image of Kit, and with her mother sober, they looked more like sisters than mother and daughter. Kit took great pride in that, obsessive about her skin care regime. The long-sleeve sweater dress Kit wore flattered and skimmed her curves. Audrey was so proud of her mother for keeping up with her sobriety. But, she was with her cousins. She did not want her mother staying in the house with them. They'd get no peace from the constant helpful advice and cleaning.

"Easy, sug. We're here to help y'all break the curse," Kit answered.

Of all the things Audrey had been expecting them to say....that was not one of them.

Audrey had expected dinner with her mother and aunts to be awkward. After all, in her thirty-two years on this Earth, the sisters had barely been able to get along. Now...they sat around her mother's antique table, cackling and sharing stories about their childhood as though everything was normal. As though they hadn't dropped a bomb on her and her two cousins. She shared a look with Ness and then Nic.

What the fuck? Ness mouthed.

Audrey shrugged and continued peeling potatoes as she'd been assigned to do. She was waiting on the shoe to drop, and it seemed her mother was just as determined not to clarify her earlier statements.

Nic sighed next to her, dropping the peas she'd been shucking. "Okay. This is torture. The four of you obviously know something you're not telling us, and the suspense is getting on my nerves."

Lauren sucked her teeth at her daughter, but Audrey was glad that Nic had said something. She was about to crawl out of her skin.

"Thank God," Ness muttered under her breath before sipping out of her glass of sweet tea.

"Hiding what, Nicole? We're here to help y'all break the curse. It's as simple as that," Dawn said.

Nic shook her head. "But it's not that simple. You four couldn't even get along for your mother's funeral, not that I got to see for myself—"

"—Jesus Christ!" Lauren snapped.

"—since I wasn't there," Nicole kept going despite her mother's outburst. "So excuse us if we're suspicious of the sudden kumbaya."

"It's not that we wouldn't welcome your help, but you have to admit, it's a little sudden," Audrey interjected to break up the coming argument.

The sisters shared a look, and Lauren sighed. "If you must know, it's because of your relationship with JT."

Nic's eyes widened. "What does my relationship have to do with it?"

"You're about to get a look at the curse first hand. If we can spare you—any of you— that, then that's what we're going to do." Lauren answered.

Shelby cleared her throat. "There were some things I left out when you had asked me about the curse. I didn't know how to tell you, Nic. You girls are stronger than us, and I was afraid it would make a difference with the timing. It's why I called your mothers."

Audrey looked to Aunt Shelby, confused. "What about the timing? If the protections are in place, then there should be no rush, right?"

Her heart rate picked up, a little in panic. She urgently wanted to break the curse, if only for her own selfish reason, but she thought she had more time to learn what she needed to do so.

"You told me that the candle and Grandmother's wards would help," Nic said.

"And they will," Shelby rushed to assure her.

"Then, what else is there?" Ness asked.

Audrey completely abandoned the potatoes and gave her family her absolute attention. Her stomach was churning because she had a feeling that what they told her would absolutely change her world.

Chapter Three

Israel eyed the small conference room. It would do for the purposes of the meeting he had in the next twenty minutes. It was a standard hotel conference room, with ugly carpet, plastic chairs lined up behind a wooden table, and no windows. His enforcers swept the room, checking for any signs of danger or eavesdropping. The three men moved in sync, and though it was something they often did, they didn't slack on the job. Eli gave him the all-clear, and Israel sat at the table to await their guest. He chose the seat facing the door.

Eli gathered the twins, his face stern. "Keep your cats on a leash unless absolutely necessary. We're on Taylor territory, which means y'all gotta keep it tight. I'm not trying to get into a war with these country ass wolves over no stupid shit."

Eli dismissed them with that word, and the twins spread out in the room.

"Eloquent," Israel murmured.

Eli scoffed and took a seat to Israel's left. "Man, Lucky. You sure about this?"

"My wife is here, and until she's at my side, this is where we'll be." Israel adjusted his tie, resolute.

He hadn't had the chance to change, so he was still in the designer suit he'd worn into the office earlier this morning. He dragged a hand through his beard and waited on their guest of honor. The wolf swaggered in minutes later. Israel frowned at the power coming off the man. He shared a look with Eli, who nodded, acknowledging the wolf's new power. Jeremiah Taylor wore a pair of jeans, a black shirt with his leather vest on top, and the insignia for his motorcycle gang blazoned across his chest. There was no hiding his affiliation; in fact, the wolf seemed proud of the fact that he belonged to a gang. Israel couldn't relate. His family would disown him altogether.

"Israel Black," The wolf said as a greeting.

"Jeremiah."

"JT's fine," he said, sitting to the right of Israel.

JT put a few chairs' distance between them but made sure to keep the door in his peripheral. His eyes scanned the room, taking note of Israel's enforcers before turning his attention back to him.

"What brings you to my part of the country?"

"You have something of mine," Israel answered.

JT looked neither surprised nor concerned. "Personally or professionally?"

Israel nodded his head and cleared the room of everyone but Eli. "My wife is here, in your territory."

JT said nothing. Taylor's silence irritated him. Israel controlled all the shifters in his territory, so to be dismissed so casually...once again, Israel wondered at the source of the wolf's new power.

"Nothing to say to that?"

"Israel, I'm here on the strength of our dealings over the years. That's it. I don't deal in subtext. Whatever you need to tell me, you gotta make it plain."

Israel pulled out his phone and scrolled over to the only picture of his wife he had. He slid the phone over to JT.

He grabbed it and whistled. "Tangled with a Fouche, huh?" JT gave him a rueful smile before sliding his phone back to him. "Welcome to the ride."

"I want her released to me," Israel told him.

The smile on JT's face dropped, the wolf from within the man peeking out. "I don't like the language, proper though it may sound. No one's holding Audrey, and furthermore, no one in this area would dare cross a Fouche."

"Her grandmother is no longer alive." He couldn't see how the Fouche name could hold that much weight with the matriarch gone.

"I can see now you ain't met my mate. Patsy didn't leave this Earth without making sure her family could handle everything that comes with the name."

Israel's eyebrows winged high, unable to contain his surprise. The wolf's mate had access to the Fouche power?

JT continued. "I don't work for you, Israel, so you not finna come onto our territory making demands. Jedidiah learned that the hard way."

Eli growled at the threat, but Israel held up his hand to silence him.

"I have my own set of enemies, JT. I cannot leave my wife here in the open."

JT studied him for long moments. "Is Audrey hiding from you?"

Israel clenched his teeth. "I'm not privy to my wife's thoughts on the matter."

JT smirked. "Such fancy words. Best I can do is tell her you're here."

Israel nodded, knowing it was as far as he could push the wolf. "I would prefer that you didn't. All I ask is that you don't...interfere."

"So long as it all remains polite, I don't see any reason for it to be my business." JT's wolf filled his gaze, the male's eyes changing to gold before darkening back to their original color.

Israel heard the underlying threat. The male was bold as hell; he could respect that.

JT stood. "These three the only ones with you?"

He nodded again, happy that he'd kept his numbers small.

JT grunted. "I got my hands full with my own Fouche. Don't come here fucking it up for all of us, hear?" With a smirk, the cocky wolf left.

Eli turned to him, "arrogant motherfucker."

"If you were toting that kind of power, you would be just as cocky."

JT got that from mating with the Fouche woman? It was interesting because it revealed something about Israel's relationship with his wife. He had gained nothing when he'd exchanged vows with Audrey. Was it because they weren't bound as mates? Was that what it took to access her powers?

And now he wanted his wife even more.

"You didn't ask him where she was," Eli reminded him.

Israel waved that off. "In a town this small, we can find out easy enough."

"What do you want to do if you're tracked here?"

"Release the temper I'm holding on to by a thread."

Until Audrey was returned to him and under his control, his patience would be thin. Israel almost wished one of his enemies would try something in his current state of mind.

Eli chuckled. "I'll look around and see what we're dealing with."

Israel's thoughts turned to Audrey, and he reached out his magic, trying once again to connect with her. Once upon a time in their marriage, the two of them had been able to touch each other's thoughts. He loathed admitting that he missed that. He closed his eyes, almost smelling her unique scent in the wind. He had to keep his purpose in the forefront of his mind. Falling in love with his wife was not part of the plan; doing so could get them both killed.

He had to remember that.

Chapter Four

As far as bombshells went, this one would rate a twelve out of ten. Maybe even a twenty. Audrey needed a little more time to process what her mother had just dropped into their laps. She built up the shields in her mind with steel, struggling with the wild magic fluttering around her family. Her mother's kitchen was tense, the magic making the air thick. It wasn't just her thoughts that were all over the place.

She breathed a sigh of relief when the last shield went up. Her head quieted, and now the only thoughts there were her own. Not that they were any less chaotic than everyone else's.

"I need you to explain this to me like I'm five," Ness finally broke the silence.

Dawn cleared her throat.

Nicole cut in before their aunt could speak. "Because it sounded to me like you said that the men we love would become obsessed with us? How does that even work?"

"Have you noticed anything strange with Jeremiah?" Aunt Shelby asked.

Nic flinched, closing her eyes. "Sometimes he goes...like, blank when I ask him to do things for me. It's like he blindly does it."

Their mothers shared a look. Kit spoke. "It's not just death and leaving that you have to worry about. They lose themselves in between. That's the real danger with the curse."

"It's like a thrall," Lauren said, shuddering. "It gradually goes away if they leave, but there is always that lingering feeling."

"Number two," Nic said.

Her aunt's second husband had stalked her when they got divorced, going so far as to threaten her life when she left. Kit had been scared for her sister, and Audrey vividly remembered all their harried three-way calls about it.

All at once, the rumors about the women in their family were starting to make sense to Audrey, and not at all in a way that felt flattering. For the most part, the men in this town avoided the Fouche women. A part of her had understood that they didn't want to end up dead, but hearing this...what person in their right mind wanted to become a zombie because they fell in love with a Fouche?

"How long did he stalk you, Aunt Lauren?" Ness asked.

"It took a year and some help from my magic."

Audrey reached out and gripped her aunt's hands. "I never realized that was part of the curse."

"Once I realized how serious Nic was about Jeremiah, I knew we had to do something. Shelby called, but I was already moving things around so that I could come down."

"So the protection spells aren't to keep them alive?" Nic asked, alarmed.

"The thralls they are in are so complete that they live for us, even to the detriment of their health," Dawn told them. "Shelby had the most luck with her protections."

"How long before the effect of the curse starts?" Audrey asked. Her thoughts immediately went to her current problem.

"The accidents happen almost right as you fall in love. Then comes the devotion," Kit said.

"How long do I have?" Nic asked.

"It varies. Mama's protection spells could last a while." Lauren told her.

"Worst case?" Nic whispered.

Lauren gave her a sympathetic look. "Maybe another year until you start to see a difference."

"But," Shelby jumped in, "remember, the girls are more powerful than us. We can't go by what happened to us. She and JT have only been mated for a few months, and she's already noticing a change."

"So it could be sooner?" Audrey asked, her mind spinning.

She thought she had more time to work on breaking the curse, but with this hanging over their head, she needed to move faster and work harder.

Kit shrugged. "It's triggered by us falling in love, but as soon as they do, the devotion starts."

"Oh God," Nic said and left the table.

Lauren looked heartbroken. "It's why we're here to help. If I can save Nicole from this, I want to."

Her heart hurt for her cousin. The guilt she felt for leaving Israel lessened as she realized what could've happened to him. But he was still looking for her. She knew it because he told her every night in her dreams. Now she wondered if it was the curse making him so determined to have her back. She shook off that depressing thought and got up to follow Nicole. She found her on the front porch staring into the woods.

Nic spoke the moment Audrey stood next to her. "All that time, I've been so flippant about her leaving her husbands, and she's been doing it for their own good. My father is still bitter, you know. So even when she leaves them, they still pine. I feel like such an asshole."

Audrey rubbed Nic's back. "Aunt Lauren understands, I'm sure. But an apology won't hurt."

Nic sighed and turned to her. "You looked equally shook. What's going on with you?"

Now was the perfect opening to tell her cousin that she'd secretly married a stranger and said stranger was now hunting her down. The words wouldn't come out, though.

Nicole held her hand up. "You ain't gotta answer, just thought I'd try and reach out. I'm new to this sharing shit anyways."

Guilt prodded her. Audrey took a deep breath and realized that her cousin was trying.

"I got into a little situationship. Hearing that part about the curse just reiterated that I was smart to get out." She told her.

Nicole nodded. "How the fuck am I going to tell JT?"

Audrey didn't have any answers for her cousin, but she prayed it worked out. If Nicole couldn't figure it out with her mate that she loved, then there was nothing left for Audrey.

Audrey cursed as she made another mistake with the spell she was working on. The directions were vague as hell, not to mention the writing was a little hard to decipher. She and Aunt Shelby were planning to re-write the pages of her great-grandmother's journals so they could read them, but she was impatient to start. Now that they didn't know when the curse would begin to affect Nicole's mating, Audrey wanted to get right on it. She didn't think there was any time to waste.

She'd barely allowed herself time for a shower when she returned from her mother's house. She'd headed straight for her grandmother's workshop to start as soon as she finished.

"Hey, Lil mama."

She looked up at JT leaning against the door frame of her workshop. Her heart started thudding because his face was so serious.

"I need to holla at you," he said.

She licked her lips and wiped her hands down her jogging pants.

She was already on alert since the conversation with her family. There was nothing about JT's visit that seemed like good news. Her magic flared out in nervousness, and his thoughts came back to her.

"No," she whispered.

He'd found her.

JT studied her. "I done told you and your cousin about all that wild magic," He gently rebuked.

"I'm sorry, I'm already on edge."

She braced for him to say aloud what she'd just discerned from his thoughts.

"I had a meeting a little bit ago with a warlock from Miami."

Her stomach dived. "What kind of meeting?" she managed.

"He said he was in town to get his wife back."

Fuck.

She wanted to run and pack, but where the hell else could she go?

"We need to handle it for you?" JT asked, his voice deep.

"I..." she swallowed. She didn't want him dead...did she? No, of course not. She shook her head.

"Talk to me, Lil mama. If you in some shit, you know we got you."

She sighed. "I made a mistake," she admitted.

"A mistake we need to take care of?" JT asked.

"No, he...we got married. It was impulsive," she admitted.

There had been something about Israel that had called to her. It could've been the drink talking, but she didn't think so. There had been plenty of time to rectify the mistake after the deed was done, except...she hadn't. Instead, she'd made it worse and caught feelings for him.

"Why'd you run from him?" JT prompted.

"I woke up and realized what I'd done. I don't even know him," she whispered.

That wasn't exactly true, but she didn't want to lay out all of her business to him. What in the hell would she do?

"He said he came back to 'retrieve you,'" JT put up air quotes. "I told him we don't play that shit around here. So if it's not what you want, just say the word."

"No, no. I'll take care of it," She said hastily. "I don't want to get y'all involved in some shit I made."

"I'll leave it alone, but if anything changes, you already know." He warned her.

Her throat clogged, and she nodded at his warning. The Taylors didn't leave problems around, and if Israel became a problem...JT and his family would likely make him and anyone who came looking for him disappear. JT walked around the table and pulled her into his arms. She loved that about shifters. Their tactile nature wouldn't allow them to let someone suffer without some kind of physical touch. She needed the hug after the day she'd had. She hugged him tightly, her cat reacting to his power. It enveloped her and reassured her. A tear escaped. She missed her daddy, no matter how many years had passed, and the fact that the Taylors had welcomed her into their brood with no questions had always reassured her.

He stepped back. "He gotta lot of power."

She refocused on him and nodded. "Yeah, he runs Miami."

"You got power, I ain't finna discount that, but he had an alpha lion with him, which means he's strong enough to call animals to him. You think I'll have an issue with him in town?"

She shrugged. "Honestly, JT, he's well known, and the shifters around him are tough, but they ain't Taylors." She smiled.

He grunted. "Ain't nobody like us, Lil mama. You gon' be alright?"

"It took me a few years after we were married to understand what I'd gotten into. I panicked and ran. But, I think I can handle it if he tries anything with me."

Probably.

"I'll stay out of it for now, then. You might want to let your cousins know before they find out from the streets." He warned.

She sighed because he was right. If Ness had to find out from someone else, she would curse her smooth out.

Chapter Five

Audrey faced the pile of papers on her desk and sighed. There was no way she was getting through any of it today. She was exhausted and aggravated. The little bit of sleep she'd been able to manage had been filled with dreams of Israel. She should've worked from home. That would've been the sensible thing to do, especially since she was ducking her husband. But, she had been working at the brewery for only six months, so it probably wouldn't look good for her to slack off.

She enjoyed her new job, and now that Uncle Brandon had turned the reins over to her—with slight supervision—she was getting into a groove. She'd taken classes in between keeping Kit out of bars, so on paper, she had a bachelor's in Business Administration. She'd initially done it to open her own tea shop, but this would do in the meantime. Now, all she had to do was redecorate Uncle Brandon's office. To that end, Ness was coming in a little before lunch to look around.

She sighed and slipped her shoes back onto her feet. It was nearing lunch, and she'd gotten next to nothing done. It had been four days since JT told her that Israel was in town, and in the subsequent days, the dreams had gotten more vivid. To the point where she woke up sweating, horny, and still feeling his arms around her. It was maddening. She laid her head down on her desk.

The other day when she'd stepped out for lunch, she thought she smelled him and panicked. All week she'd brought her lunch to work to avoid possibly seeing him in the streets. It wasn't sustainable, but it was all she could think to do. Today though, was the weekly lunch she had with her cousins, so she couldn't avoid it. Maybe she should change the venue to Lore. Surely Israel wouldn't be bold enough to walk into a wolf-shifter bar? Even he wouldn't be that reckless.

She looked up as the door to her office opened, expecting to see her assistant. Instead, it was the man who had been haunting her dreams. She whipped open her desk drawer and pulled out her gun, standing up quickly. Greedily, she took him in. His deep mahogany skin matched the brown plaid of his suit and contrasted with the crisp white shirt he wore underneath. God, the way that man filled out a suit. It was tailored to fit his tall, muscular frame to a T. His cologne filled the room, and Audrey wanted to close her eyes and bask in it.

Her eyes traced his face, noting the thicker beard that now matched his thick dark eyebrows. His narrow, hooded eyes studied her just as hard as she did him. He licked his full lips, and she clamped her mouth tightly so as not to mimic the motion.

His hair was longer than when she last saw it, curling into locs at the top but still in a low fade on the sides. The locs were new, half-hearted, still not heavy or organized enough to fall down. So many changes since she'd last seen him. His presence was still dark, power-ful, and though she didn't want to admit it...intimidating.

"What are you doing here?"

His smile showed off his perfect white teeth. "My wife is here. What do you mean?"

Her heart started racing. "I left you."

"You snuck out."

"Semantics. Take it up with your grandmother," She snapped.

There was a small imperceptible...something... that flashed through his eyes. Audrey didn't have time to decipher what it meant.

"She's irrelevant to this conversation and has nothing to do with what's between us." He said after a pause.

"There is no us. Not anymore."

He chuckled. "I beg to differ."

He stepped further into her office and closer to her desk. He paused and gave her a devastating smile as she switched the safety off on her gun.

"Now that we're in the same room, I can feel you. Just minutes in your presence, and our heartbeats are synching. Surely you don't plan to pretend we don't affect each other?"

Damn him, it was true.

"You need to leave. There's nothing for you here." She told him.

"You're here, Audrey," he said calmly, his voice moving through her like warm molasses.

She growled. Israel said it as though that explained everything. As though she was overreacting. That irritated her because she couldn't be sure she wasn't. And instead of talking to someone about it, she'd pretended he didn't exist.

"Talk to me, sweetheart. Surely we can work out whatever had you running scared."

She steadied her hand. "That's not happening."

"You would pull a gun out on your husband?" He stepped closer. "You promised yourself to me. Have you forgotten?"

"I will shoot you without a second thought, Israel. I'm not going back with you."

He sighed. "I actually believe you would shoot me." He smiled, and her clit thumped. "That shouldn't turn me on, but I'm afraid it does, Kitten."

She cursed as a shudder of longing shook her body.

"You lied to me and tricked me into marrying you." She needed the conversation back on track.

He scoffed, "I don't see how I coerced you into anything. You could've said no at any time during that night. Not after the first nor seventh orgasm did I have to force you into anything. You're a big girl, Kitten."

She flinched at the reminder even as her skin heated.

"You could've told me what you really wanted from me, but you didn't." She hissed.

He didn't deny that—couldn't really—but as far as he was concerned, that was easily forgiven. Or at least, he would've thought so before Audrey pulled the gun out on him. He licked his lips and traced his eyes over his wife's body. She was beautiful, even with the signs of exhaustion on her face. Her doe eyes were dark underneath, which was noticeable since she didn't wear much makeup. She'd cut her hair and changed the color since he'd last seen her. It was a dark pink color that matched well with her caramel skin. Even her brows were the same color. Her lush lips had a simple gloss on them that made them shine. He wanted to kiss it off.

The door opened, interrupting them, and a powerful woman walked in. She favored Audrey enough that he knew it was one of her cousins. The woman went to Audrey's side; her head cocked to the side as she examined him.

"Didn't know you had company, cousin," she said dryly.

Israel gritted his teeth in aggravation. "I locked that door."

"With a little more than the mechanism on it," the woman admitted, a cocky smile tilting her lips.

"Everything's fine, Ness," Audrey told her.

Her cousin didn't say anything about the gun starting to shake in Audrey's hand, which was interesting to him. Ness didn't look concerned with the whys.

"We got a problem here?"

Israel studied Ness the way a scientist would examine a sample. The woman had broken through his lock spell. He was curious to know how long it had taken her. She carried all that Fouche power better than his wife. Or rather, she seemed more confident with it. In the years he'd been with Audrey, he'd only seen her suppress her magic. He wanted to explore the difference between the two women. But, with the look Audrey was giving him, that wouldn't be any time soon.

"I'm giving you to the count of five, Israel, and then I'm pulling the trigger."

"Nah, give his ass three," Ness taunted. "I don't trust him."

Interesting indeed.

Israel put his hands up. "I'll see you again, Wife."

Using that title seemed to irritate Audrey more. Which probably meant she hadn't told her cousins about them. He smiled and backed from the room. Chasing his wife down was aggravating, yes, but he had to admit...

That shit was fun too.

He met Eli at the bar of the small brewery, smiling at the employee giving him a taste of the beers.

"How'd it go?" His friend asked, his eyebrow raised.

"About how you predicted," he admitted.

"I told you that woman don't play that shit. You hard-headed, Lucky," Eli preceded him out the door, his gaze watchful as they got into the rental.

"She's hard-headed, not me."

Eli laughed. "Yeah, aight. What you wanna do now?"

Israel gave his friend a smile that had him shaking his head. "Feel like a drink tonight?"

Eli gave him an incredulous look. "You hell, Iz. You ain't gone be satisfied until you start some shit."

"Clearly, my wife wants to see me show my ass. Otherwise, she'd be where she's supposed to be. It's not my fault." Israel told him.

Besides, there were only a few places where he'd be able to get to her; unfortunately, that biker bar was one of them. He would've gladly approached her at her grandmother's house...if he'd been able to get through the ward on the property. Her grandmother had a hell of a lot of power because he'd sent Eli scouting several times, and each time he and his enforcers returned saying they couldn't even locate the place. Yesterday he'd sat in the car outside the wards over the Fouche property staring at the spell to look for weak spots. Finding none after an hour, he'd given up to keep from being caught. Hence his current visit to his wife at her new job.

He scoffed.

She got a job as though she planned to stay here...away from him. Hell no, he wouldn't allow it. He glanced back at the building as they pulled off, smiling. Eli was wrong. He wasn't in it to start trouble. Israel just wanted his wife back. If it took a little trouble to accomplish that, then he was with it.

Chapter Six

Audrey sighed as Ness cut her another scathing look as they walked down the street to the café. She was so happy to see Nicole had grabbed an outdoor table. She didn't imagine Ness would be discreet when she loosed her temper.

Nic waved as she saw them. "Lord, why y'all look like that?"

Vanessa said nothing, just sat at the table and waved down a waitress.

"I ordered for you two. It should be here soon," Nic said, her gaze bouncing between her and Ness.

Audrey gratefully collapsed into her seat.

"What's wrong?" Nic asked again, sitting straight.

Ness turned her attention to the approaching waitress. "I want a whiskey neat, please." She turned her attention back to Nicole. "Audrey here has been holding out on us."

"That's not surprising," Nic said, her brows furrowed.

"Hey!" Audrey protested but then sat back because, duh, that was true.

"Right," Ness snapped.

"What's happened?"

"Audrey's husband showed up," Ness said.

Nic snorted. "Situation-ship, huh?"

Audrey sighed and drank out of the water cup in front of her.

"Oh, so she told you?" Ness asked, her face pinched in aggravation.

"Not in details, no. She just said she was dealing with some shit. Was he powerful?" Nic addressed the question to Ness.

"Hell yeah, and fine as fuck."

Audrey growled.

"Excuse you. Not you getting offended behind some dick you ain't even want to claim a second ago." Ness fussed.

"I wasn't not claiming him. I just...it's complicated." Audrey muttered.

"How long has it been complicated?" Nic was significantly less peeved than Ness.

Audrey's cheeks burned. "Four years."

"Four years. Four?" Ness snapped.

Audrey's stomach churned, and she put her head down. "It was an impulsive thing."

"Biitch," Ness said. "Oh, baby girl, you just saved her life." She told the waitress, grabbing her drink.

Nic snickered. "Why weren't we invited to the wedding?"

"We hadn't talked in years, and I don't know...everything happened so fast. We flew to Vegas." Audrey moved her head so the waitress could put down their food.

Nic had ordered her a club sandwich, and she was grateful. She was hungry, and the sandwiches from this place were her new favorite thing.

"So, a whirlwind, then. I understand," Nic said.

Ness scoffed. "Nicole, you gotta be shitting me. She got a whole damn husband. A dangerous one, I might add."

Nic took a bite of her salad. "Let me shut up then, chile, because you mad mad."

"Why aren't you more upset?" Ness asked, not touching her food.

"She's right, Vanessa. Our communication had been very lax up until recently. We hadn't seen each other in years. What, you expected to be maid of honor?"

"*Your* communication. Not ours," Ness said, waving her hand between herself and Audrey. She got up from the table. "You know what, fuck this. I thought we were closer than this, Audrey. Guess I was stupid."

"Ness," Audrey called after her, but her cousin ignored her, not once slowing her pace.

Nic sighed. "She drove, so..."

Audrey laughed. She couldn't help it. Nic smiled and reached across the table.

"Are you okay?"

"I mean, I don't know."

Nic went back to her food. "Are you scared of him?"

"I pulled a gun on him when he showed up at the office," she said quietly.

Nic's eyes bucked. "That is...wow. That doesn't answer the question, though."

She rubbed her temples. "I don't know. I may have overreacted. He's just so overwhelming and exciting." And sexy and addicting, but she kept that last thought to herself. "On top of that, he has some kind of family baggage that I'm not sure I want to be involved in."

Nic snorted. "Ain't no way you talking about family baggage."

That stung but was accurate. Their family had their own baggage that also affected her decisions regarding Israel.

"Israel is a lot to handle, and I don't know that I'm up to the task," she admitted.

Nic studied her for a long moment. "Is he worth it?"

Audrey shrugged because she wasn't sure about that just yet. Especially given what she'd found out about him.

"You want me to tell JT?"

"He already knows," Audrey admitted.

"Wait a damn minute." Nic whipped her phone out. "Ok, now I'm perturbed. JT knows you're married and didn't tell me."

Audrey held her hand up. "I told him not to say anything."

Nic squinted at her but put her phone down. She had a feeling she'd just delayed the cussing JT would get for keeping a secret from his mate. They went back to eating. The quiet between them wasn't strained, and Audrey took a deep breath. There was something calming about Nicole's unflappable nature. She'd once thought of it as apathetic, but the more time she spent with her cousin, she realized it just took a lot to fluster Nicole. She had a well of calm that Audrey really appreciated at the moment.

Ness stormed back to the table and took her seat. She started eating as though nothing untoward had just happened. Audrey hid her smile. Ness was quick to blow up, but it passed just as fast.

"Did the tantrum help?" Nic asked offhand.

"Why are you so goddamned mean?" Ness grumbled.

Audrey and Nic both snickered.

Chapter Seven

Israel was happy with the hoodie he wore underneath his leather bomber as he stepped out of the SUV onto the gravel lot of Lore. It was cold as hell outside. It made him miss his Miami penthouse all the more. Florida in January was nothing like Georgia. He adjusted the olive green khakis pants, dropping the hem of them into the dark brown leather boots he wore. He was dressed down on purpose, knowing exactly the way Audrey liked to see him. He adjusted the diamond-studded watch and smirked as Eli cursed next to him.

"Let me do the talking. If you go in there with that bougie shit, we liable be jumped." Eli warned him.

Israel laughed. "Fuck you. I'm not worried about these country ass wolves."

Eli sighed and turned to address the twins. "Act like you got some sense when we go in here. We just here to start a little shit and maybe have a drink. If it goes sideways, just make sure Lucky don't kill a bunch of people."

The twins nodded at Eli's instruction. Israel didn't bother taking offense at his friend's orders. He could control himself...maybe. It would all depend on how his wife acted. The four of them headed inside. Eli growled when they were stopped at the door. The bouncer patted them down, clearly looking for weapons. Eli's eyes widened when the bouncer reached into his jacket pocket. The gun that should've been there was now a wad of cash. Israel had switched the contents of Eli's pockets with his own, and his best friend's gun was now weighing heavy in his pants pocket. Israel was cocky, yes, but going inside Taylor headquarters without holding something was just stupid. It took only a little bit of magic to move their weapons around as the bouncer did his job. Once he was finished searching them, the wolf reluctantly allowed them to enter.

Though he'd easily gotten through the door, they were met with resistance once inside. Immediately they were surrounded, the crowd going silent as they looked on to see what was happening. Israel looked around until he spotted Audrey at a back table with her cousins. He smiled as her eyes widened. He liked her new short hair. The bangs swooped across her forehead, framing her beautiful face. It made her eyes stand out. She wore a simple tank top and still managed to look amazing. He couldn't look away. Dante, JT's Beta, pushed through the crowd and stood in Eli's face.

"The fuck a bunch of cats want in here?" Dante asked.

Israel ignored them all and focused his magic on Audrey. He probed her mind until he found an opening. Sliding in quickly, he felt her surprise.

"I want to talk, kitty cat." He spoke to her telepathically, happy that he could still do it even after all their time apart.

He could feel her frustration. *"Why? I said what I had to say earlier. You need to leave."*

Israel smirked and started gathering magic from the air around them. He swirled it around in his hands, taunting her. *"You and I both know what I can do, kitten. Give me a few minutes, and I'll behave."*

"Fuck you, Lucky. Leave." She used her power to push him from her mind, slamming up a shield.

That was fine by him. He could show her better than he could tell her. The lights flickered, and grumbles started around the room. Next, the bottles that hung from the ceiling as light fixtures began swaying.

"I thought this place was supposed to be neutral." Eli taunted the Beta.

JT walked through the crowd as they parted around him. "I don't know why the fuck you thought that."

The tension tightened, and in response, the enforcer next to him lifted his shirt, showing off his gun. Israel internally cursed. Eli was not so restrained. The sounds of racking shotguns and the clink of weapons sounded all around them.

JT gave them a sinister smile that showed off his alpha wolf power. The male's canines lowered. "Our shit bangs too, playboy."

They were at a stand-off. Israel cranked his power until the liquor bottles behind the bar started rattling. The crowd around him began murmuring, some of them pacing, unsettled by his magic. Audrey looked around in alarm.

"Fine! Just...don't wreck this place." She slammed into his mind, her anger a hot lash.

Israel smiled and drew his magic back into himself. He signaled for his enforcer to put away his weapon. He stepped next to Eli. Now that she agreed to talk to him, he needed to diffuse the situation enough so they wouldn't get kicked out.

"We're just here to have a drink, nothing more." Israel soothed.

He wanted to add magic to his voice, but something told him that would just set their Alpha off more. JT eyed him with suspicion.

"Y'all came all the way from that bougie ass island hotel to have a drink here." He crossed his arms over his chest.

Eli shrugged. "Heard the food was good too."

JT's lips twitched in amusement. He looked toward Audrey. She bit her lip, casting a look Israel's way. He worked hard to keep the smirk off his face. No call in pissing her off when they had a club full of guns pointed their way. Though, he could probably manage to protect himself and his people. After a few more tense moments, she nodded. JT held up a hand, and the air around them relaxed, the guns and weapons sliding back into their hiding spots.

"Don't start no shit, won't be no shit," JT warned them.

"Noted," Israel said.

He and his enforcers walked over to the bar, and the bartender gave them a warm smile. It was an amused smile that let him know, despite their initial welcome, no one would fuck with them. He and Eli sat while the other two flanked them, their eyes on the crowd behind them.

"What can I get for y'all?" She asked.

"Your oldest bourbon," Eli ordered. "He's paying."

Israel snickered and nodded. She pulled a bottle out from the bottom of the bar and poured them each a drink. She glanced back at the two enforcers at his back.

"And them?"

"The twins aren't drinking. They're on duty," Israel told her.

She frowned. "They don't look like twins."

"Aww, now, lil baby, you gon' hurt their feelings," Eli said, his voice lowering.

Israel shook his head. His friend was always on bullshit when it came to women.

She snorted and waved off his flirting. "I like excitement as much as the next person, but I ain't trying to be in here late cleaning up, so stay out of trouble, hear," were her parting words.

Eli chuckled and lifted his drink. "Lucky, you play too much," he muttered and downed the contents of his glass. Israel smirked at his best friend.

"Don't act like you aren't having fun," he taunted.

"Now, when Audrey slaps the shit out of you, don't come over here expecting sympathy," Eli told him.

Israel laughed, relaxing for the first time in a while. Maybe it was the bar, or it could've been the fact that Audrey was near. Whatever it was, he ordered another round. Eli passed him a blunt, and they both lit up.

"Aye, you gotta send ol' boy back to Miami. He way too scary to roll with us," his best friend said with a shake of his head.

Israel eyed the guard and agreed. "Did I not tell you that when you assigned him. We get into way too much shit. Send him back on the first flight out."

"I'ma send his ass back on Spirit," Eli grumbled. "Out here got us looking soft as hell."

"That's cold, man," Israel said, chuckling.

He spun his stool around and looked around the room. It was full of wolf shifters, their earthy power filling the place. In all that, he could feel the energy from Audrey and her cousins. The coolness of their magic sliced through the air. He could see the difference in their abilities. The woman from earlier, Ness, the frigidness of her power probably meant that she had some experience with necromancy and could undoubtedly deal with spirits. It contrasted with the third cousin. Her magic danced around her warm and sweet, which meant she likely dealt with natural elements. He turned his attention to his wife and sighed in longing. Her magic danced around her wilder than what it was when he last saw her. He knew first-hand how clever she was at wielding spells. It seemed like being home again had amped her power even more.

The greedy part of him was excited about that.

She was doing her best to avoid looking at him, which was fine by him. He would look his fill. From his current position, he could see that what he thought was a tank top was a whole dress. The red fabric clung to her slight curves, her handful of breasts just perfect for him. Her hair matched the dress to perfection, the red lipstick she wore enticing him from way across the room. Jesus, his wife was sexy as hell.

She stood and took off for what he could assume was the bathroom. She disappeared down a hallway, and he stood to follow after her. He put a hand on Eli's shoulder to let him know he would be back. He tugged on his ear in warning, and Eli nodded, understanding that he would be out of communication for a bit. Israel slid through the crowd, chanting under his breath and gathering just enough magic for a small dampening spell. By the time he got into the hallway where Audrey had disappeared, the noise level around him was minimal. Satisfied the spell would hold, he posted up on the wall across from the only door in the hallway.

It only took a few minutes until she came out. Her eyes widened a moment before a resigned look covered her face. His heart beat erratically in his chest. He slid his trembling hands into his pants pockets, otherwise, the temptation to touch her would override his good sense. She tried to walk past him, but he stepped into her way.

"Israel."

She sighed his name, and it took his breath away. The silence of the hallway pressed around them, the heat between them thickening the air. He stepped closer to her. The hitch in her breathing satisfied him deeply.

Unable to resist, he pulled his hand out of his pocket and cupped her cheek. "How have you been, my love?"

"I'm not your love anymore."

He scoffed. "You'll always be that. Why did you leave me?"

Audrey sucked her teeth and slid her face from his hand. "Oh, she didn't brag about it? Funny."

He frowned, not knowing what she meant. "Who are you...." he paused. There was only one woman she could've been referencing. "My grandmother did something to you?"

"She told me why you married me."

He clenched his jaw. Of all the reasons he'd thought of for why she'd run, that hadn't crossed his mind. Especially since Audrey was right and his grandmother hadn't bragged. Annabelle could never resist taunting him.

. . .

48

Audrey's heart hurt with him so close. She wanted to trace the scar beneath his eye as she'd done so many times before. He leaned forward until their mouths were millimeters apart. They were sharing air, and her heart was thumping. Her stomach fluttered in nervousness. He was wearing her down and not just in the hallway. The visits to her dreams, the popping up. All of it was pretty effective in battering through her defenses.

"Whatever she told you had to be a lie." He leaned down and kissed her lightly. "I've missed you, kitten."

She needed to put more space between them. He was stealing the very breath from her.

"She told me you came after me for my family's power."

He flinched, and her heart broke all over again. Especially when he didn't deny it. She could've used her magic and prodded his mind to see what he was thinking, feeling...but that way lay danger. Just the brief contact they'd had earlier had her mind and body reaching out to him for more. It was nearing the full moon, so the power from her cat even reacted to Israel.

He got on her damn nerves!

"You need to leave before the Taylors really get mad. This is not a place for you."

"Is that why you ran here? You thought they would keep me from you?" His thumb caressed her bottom lip.

Her heart raced. Israel was serious, deadly; she knew that.

"If anything happens to my family or them, I'll never forgive you." She whispered.

"And now you plead for them?" He tsked. "Come back to me, my love, and nothing has to happen."

Power swelled in her chest at the threat. She squinted her eyes, looking for the telltale signs of his spellwork. The amount of noise in the hallway didn't match what it was when she walked into the bathroom, so she knew he had done something. Spotting the shimmer of his power in the corner, she worked to dismantle it. She wanted to jump in triumph when it dissipated. All at once, noise flooded the hallway, the smells from the bar scented the air, and she could sense her cousins again.

Pride for the work she'd been doing filled her, and from the shine in his eyes, Israel was impressed and not hiding it. She sighed, and she stepped around him.

"As I've said, there's no us. There's me, stupidly catching feelings, and there's you, playing in my fucking face."

She took a deep breath and walked back as calmly as she could to the table with her cousins.

Ness noticed her face immediately. "What's wrong?"

"I'm ready to go." She grabbed her coat off the back of the chair where she had been sitting.

She didn't need to say anything else. Nic chugged her beer and stood, and Ness was right behind her as they made their way to the door. Nic stopped and spoke with her mate, exchanging a deep kiss.

JT looked at Audrey. "You good?"

She nodded.

His eyes raked across her face. "Need me to call Unc on him?"

She smiled as he intended. JT had multiple uncles, and either one of them could do damage.

"Call me when you get home, love," he told Nic.

The closer she got to the door, the more she wanted to look behind her. She could feel Israel's gaze on her. She stopped walking as she felt him prod her mind. She'd been shocked at the first touch of his mind when he'd entered the bar. It had been months since she'd felt him. She let him in and closed her eyes at the emotions that swamped her.

"I'll let you sleep."

Her heart tripped, and her throat clogged. She was conflicted. In her dreams was the only time she got to see him and let her guard down...if only a little. Would she miss him? She brushed through his mind for one last lingering taste before slamming down the shields over her thoughts. It was for the best.

The car ride to the house was quiet. They all groaned when they saw the car in the yard.

"Which one do you think it is?" Audrey asked.

Ness shook her head. "Is there a preferable answer to that question?"

Nic snorted. "Nope."

They got out, and unfortunately, it was all the sisters. The four of them were piled into her grandmother's workshop, huddling over the journals they had found in her grandmother's safe while investigating her murder.

"I ain't never seen y'all get along this well," Nic grumbled for the doorway.

Audrey shook her head and laughed. Her cousin was so damn mean. They all gave her varying alarming looks.

"You've been messing with the andisa plant?" Shelby asked.

Audrey frowned. "I don't know what that is."

Kit looked panicked. "The amplifier, you've been making spells with it? Have you been helping her grow it, Nicole?"

"Woah," Nic said. "I don't even know what y'all are talking about."

The sisters looked at each other before Kit turned to Shelby. "Was mama doing it?"

Shelby shrugged. "I know mama was working to break the curse, but she didn't share everything."

"What's the andisa plant?" Ness asked, leaning over their shoulder.

Kit looked at Dawn, who gave a panicked look to Lauren and Shelby.

Lauren sighed. "We have to tell them."

"Not tonight," Kit whispered. "I need to think about this." She left the room, and Audrey was confused.

She started to go after her mother, but Dawn stopped her.

"I got her."

The women packed up and left without telling them anything. She and her cousins shared a look.

"What was that about?" Nic asked.

Audrey shrugged, "I don't know, and I don't have the spoons." She headed towards the stairs.

"You want to talk about it?" Ness called after her.

"Not tonight," she echoed her mother's words.

Chapter Eight

Israel wiped a hand down his face and worked to quell his frustration. It had been days since he'd last laid eyes on Audrey. He wanted to continue his pursuit, but an emergency had come up, and he was needed back in Miami. It seemed the people underneath him couldn't function when he wasn't standing over them watching them. He drummed his fingertips along the top of his desk and stared at his acquisitions manager. Sullivan's tan skin was tinged red, his straight hair slicked back from his patrician face.

"So, explain it to me as though your life was on the line." Israel finally broke the silence between them.

Sullivan swallowed and looked to the right of them, towards Eli.

Israel shook his head. "I know you all count on Elijah to control me, but you'll be ass out in this instance."

Eli chuckled. *"You on one."* He told Israel telepathically.

Israel shrugged and continued to stare down at the manager.

"Edward wants more money." Sullivan spat out nervously.

"He's already agreed to the sale."

He would've paid more money. The company was worth it, but it was about the principal. They'd already drafted contracts with the agreed-upon sales price. Israel debated whether or not the company was worth the hassle. He planned to gut it of the assets he needed and some of their patents, and he would sell the rest. It would be a lucrative deal for him.

Sullivan licked his lips. "He threatened to go to the SEC and claim you coerced him with magic."

"Now see what doing it your way gets me?" Israel told Eli.

His friend shook his head. *"It was worth a try."*

Israel couldn't fault his friend. Eli had been his moral compass for so many years, keeping him from going too far. Every now and then, Israel liked to switch it up and try to conduct his business fairly and legally. But then he ended up with shit like this.

"If he reneges on the deal he signed, he will have to deal with a lot worse than magic. I'm taking control of that company at the end of this month, whether it be a smooth transition according to the contracts he's signed or if I come in there and tear shit up. Tell Edward those are his options." Israel stated.

Sullivan looked more nervous. "And if he goes to the SEC?"

"Then I'll give you a head start to get out of town."

Sullivan gulped and paled. Sweat dotted his brow. "I can't control—"

"It's your job to ensure the companies we acquire don't pull last minute shit like this. I shouldn't have to come down here and stand over your shoulder. You're useless to me if you can't manage this job independently." Israel was done talking about it. His next steps would hurt for all involved.

"Yes sir," Sullivan answered swiftly, understanding that he had reached the end of his boss' rope.

"You're dismissed."

Sullivan scrambled from the chair and left the office.

Israel turned his chair and looked at Eli, stretched out on the sofa in his office.

He raised his hands. "Now, had you used magic, he would've had a case when he went to the SEC. I just saved you an ass load of fines. You're welcome."

Israel sucked his teeth and turned back to the paperwork on his desk that needed signatures before he could head back to Georgia. All of it could've been sent to him at his hotel, but since he was already in the office, he wanted to get it done before returning. As always, his mind went back to the bar and his interaction with Audrey. It had felt good to touch her mind and renew that intimacy, even if she blocked him afterward. He reached out to her and growled when he could not sense her.

He cursed when his phone rang. From the ringtone, he was prepared to be aggravated.

"Grandmother," he greeted dryly.

"Israel, I've heard the most disappointing news."

He shook his head and rolled his shoulders. "I wasn't aware anything I did was of any business of yours."

"While you are the family vas, everything you do is our business." She snapped.

"And what have you been told?" he asked through gritted teeth.

"You let the Fouche girl escape."

"My wife has not escaped."

"Then the rumors of you chasing her to Georgia are not true?"

Instant fury swamped him. He tugged on the mental tie he had for his enforcers, calling them to him. "Is there a reason you've called me, Grandmother?"

Eli quickly left the sofa and stood at his side, a frown covering his face.

"I want the girl's power. I've given you enough time."

"And as I've told you, Audrey is mine, and I have no plans on sharing."

"You renewed the covenant for this family. It's your resp—"

"I know my responsibility!"

"The covenant requires sacrifice, Israel. Arianne depends on–"

"You won't be able to hold Arianne over my head forever." Israel nodded his head towards his office door when he heard knocking.

Eli opened the door and let in the four shifters he'd called to him.

His grandmother was still going. "You are the vas. You owe this family power, and I will hold you to the covenant."

"I know my duties."

He had voluntarily become the family vas, or vessel. He held the key to all the family magic within himself and was responsible for keeping their covenant with the goddess who granted them that magic. He knew his damn responsibility. It wasn't as though Annabelle ever let him forget it.

"Drain the girl. I won't tell you again. If I have to do it..." she let the threat hang and hung up.

Israel cursed and threw his phone. Some part of him searched for regret or hurt that Annabelle only saw him as something to be used, but he couldn't muster it up. He'd long ago given up letting her hurt him. All that was left was an impotent anger that he couldn't purge, no matter how far up he ascended in his life.

There was nothing left for Annabelle but hate. As far as he was concerned, his mother's death lay solely at his grandmother's feet. She'd forced his mother to get pregnant and have Arianne even though doctors had already advised them both of the dangers. Annabelle wanted a girl, and she'd made no bones about making sure Israel knew. Until he'd become the family's vas, she hadn't had more than a few words to say to him.

And now she was calling often, and it seemed, had spies on his team. He stared at his enforcers in front of him. Only a few knew his movements, and the four that did were lined up.

"Someone on our team has been talking out of turn."

Eli's eyes widened, and he turned to study the group. Israel trusted Eli with his life and knew he would never voluntarily talk to his grandmother. The twins were trustworthy simply because they'd proven it on multiple occasions. Even though he'd sent one home early, he didn't question their fidelity. He turned to the other two.

One guarded the front of the building, and the other was his driver when he was in town. The enforcers gave him panicked looks because they understood what could happen.

"Which of you is in contact with my grandmother?" He pushed through their minds, seeing the truth for himself.

His magic filled him, and he was ready to strike out. He made the person step forward, and the cougar who was his chauffeur shook with fear.

"It won't happen again."

"I'm very aware of that," Israel said and struck.

The cougar's back bowed, and he shifted into his animal as commanded by Israel's power. The whole process was painful, and he made sure that it was. While the cougar writhed in pain, he turned his attention to the remaining enforcers.

"I shouldn't have to tell you how much I value discretion. There'll be no other warning after this."

They nodded their understanding, staring at the writhing cat.

Israel ended the chauffeur's life, already mentally shifting through his employees for a replacement. With a simple spell, he lit the carcass on fire, turning it to ash. His next spell gathered the ashes into a neat pile for the cleaning crew to deal with. He stared at the other enforcers, and they scrambled out of his office, understanding that they were dismissed.

Eli sighed. "And what else did Annabelle want?"

"My grandmother knows we've been to Georgia."

"Should I cover Audrey when we get back?"

He sighed in frustration. JT could be a problem, but his wife was more important than anything else. She was still out from underneath his protection, but sending Eli to watch her would give him some peace of mind. He nodded his head.

"Make sure it's known she's protected and by who." He grabbed his bag and stood. "No rebuke about letting people learn from their mistakes?"

Eli snorted. "Nah, you know my motto."

"'Never let a motherfucker who knows where you lay your head betray you.'" Israel quoted by rote.

Eli nodded. "Never forget that. The jet's ready; let's go. The sooner you get Audrey back, the better for us."

Israel agreed. Unfortunately, his wife proved to be much more stubborn than he thought.

Chapter Nine

Audrey leaned against the grocery cart and stifled another groan. Her cat was getting restless because the full moon was tonight. She usually never left the house this time of the month, but Kit was dragging her around town for errands. She swallowed a growl as Kit read the label on yet another package of brown rice.

"Mama, my God, do you plan on closing this store?"

Kit cut her a side-eye. "This place don't close until ten."

It was barely after five in the evening, but because of the time of year, it felt a lot later than it was. Besides, they'd been out all damn day as Kit got supplies for her extended stay. It had been on the tip of Audrey's tongue to ask her mother how long she planned on staying, but she let it go. She didn't ask questions she didn't want to answer herself. From the amount of stuff Kit had bought, it looked like her mama had plans to move back in...permanently.

On the surface, she had no problem with that. But, a sober Kit was a very observant Kit, and that meant Audrey needed to tell her mother about Israel before the woman went looking for answers herself. She would tell her mother soon.

If only they could get out of this grocery store...

"Mama."

Kit gave her an aggrieved sigh and put the rice in the cart. "Have you tried the meditations I've sent you? You can't be snapping on people like this every full moon."

Audrey swallowed her retort because she wasn't trying to have Kit in here showing her ass, but by God, that woman was trying it. She turned her head and frowned because she could've sworn...

She did see him!

"Because, of course, this night could get worse," she muttered. "I see you, Eli," she said aloud.

"I'm not hiding, Audrey," he mocked, coming around the corner.

He was as handsome as his best friend, though his brown skin was a few shades lighter than Israel's. Elijah also kept his hair in a low fade, the waves immaculate at all times. His beard was neat and trimmed, framing his full lips. Like most cat-shifters, his body was lithe and muscular, and he moved with a grace that was sexy to watch.

Kit turned and gave him her attention. "And who is this?"

Fuck. Her mother's eyes lit with curiosity. She needed to tell Kit about Israel and soon.

"A friend," she gritted out.

Eli's smile let her know he was finna be on some bullshit.

She grabbed his arm. "I'll be right back, mama."

"I'm finna check out. Don't take too long. You don't want them waiting on you to close." Kit mocked.

Audrey rolled her eyes and dragged Eli around the corner to another aisle. "I'm not going to him. I don't care who he sends."

"I'm not here for that, Audrey." He held his hands up.

"The hell are you here for then?"

"You know Lucky's lifestyle," was all he said, and that told her everything.

"No one can get to me here." She knew of his enemies, but they were protected in Springbrook.

"His grandmother knows he's here." He warned.

She shuddered because the woman was evil, and no matter how hard she tried, she couldn't find it in herself to see past her initial impression. She'd never forget the cold perfection of her. From the designer clothes she'd worn to the understated but elegant hair and makeup, Annabelle had exuded old-fashioned charm. In contrast to her clothes, nothing about his grandmother's power was understated. It screamed loud and took up the very air in any room the woman walked in.

Audrey shuddered at the memory. "I'll be careful," she promised reluctantly.

"All the same, kitty cat, you know how he is."

She growled. "Quit calling me that shit. And you can't be following me around, Eli. This town is too damn small, and talk will start."

He shrugged, and she knew that once Israel gave orders, that was the end of it.

"Shit," she cursed and walked off, knowing he would follow her.

She pulled out her phone and dialed JT.

"What up, Lil mama."

"Just giving you a heads up, Israel put security on me."

"What you wanna do?"

She chewed her bottom lip. Why was she giving Israel any concessions? He didn't own her and she...fuck. She needed to quit lying to herself. She still cared for him. And she didn't want to be one more albatross around his neck. She'd spent the time they'd been apart getting stronger, but she knew she wasn't a match for the type of enemies Israel made.

"He's fine. I just didn't want you to be caught unawares and disappear him."

JT chuckled, and Eli snorted behind her. "You got it, Lil mama." He hung up, and she pinched the bridge of her nose.

She texted the cousin's group chat.

Audrey: Bringing company home.

Nic: Oooh, bitch, you bringing the husband home?

Ness: Oh, this gone be good.

It was finna be a mess, but she didn't have any other choices. Unless she wanted Israel following her himself, Eli would have to do. She found her mother at the checkout.

"Eli is joining us for dinner."

Kit raised an eyebrow but said nothing to her. She did, however, give Eli a charming smile.

A mess.

"Please, let me," Eli pulled out a black card and paid for her mother's groceries. Kit simpered and shot Audrey a pleased look.

"Home training, that's a plus," Kit cooed.

"Mama, please," Audrey said.

Eli laughed and helped them load the car. He slid into the back seat, and they headed back to her mother's house. Audrey chewed her bottom lip the whole ride back. How was she going to pull this off? She let her mother get out first and turned to Eli.

"Don't say shit, and follow my lead."

He smirked and got out, not agreeing, which really didn't bode well for her. He helped Kit with the groceries inside. Nic and Ness both gave her amused looks as she entered her mother's house. Ness's ass even had a bag of popcorn. Lord God, why was her family so damn messy?

"Everyone, this is Eli, Audrey's secret man," Kit introduced.

Nic snickered, and Audrey braced herself as her aunts all perked up.

"A secret man?" Lauren spoke first. "Interesting."

Dawn squinted. "Not just a man, a lion. Good for you, niece."

"There is nothing between us," she hastily reassured them.

"So that's not the man you're hiding," Aunt Shelby spoke up.

Nic was right. All this getting along shit was getting on her last nerve. Audrey shot her gaze to Ness, who shrugged, and Nic shook her head quickly. They hadn't told the aunts anything. She licked her lips and stalled, wondering what the aunts knew.

"Don't bother lying, chile. We seen the jar," Dawn said.

Audrey cleared her throat. "No, he's not the man, and that's all I'm saying about it."

"I work for her husband. I don't know what the jar is. It could be for him, though," Eli said with a smirk.

Oh, that motherfucker!

Audrey wanted to slap that smile off his face. She knew Israel had put him up to it. Damn him. All eyes shot to her.

"Husband!" Kit said, dropping the groceries she was pulling out of the bag.

Aunt Lauren laughed in delight. "Audrey, no way in hell I expected a secret husband from you. Vanessa, yes—"

"Don't do me, Auntie Lauren." Ness cut in.

"—even my daughter, but not you. You're more responsible than the two of them combined." Lauren finished.

"Hey!" Nic defended herself.

Dawn nodded her head. "Kudos for stepping out on the wild side."

Kit looked at her sisters. "I know y'all done lost your minds. Ain't no kudos. What were you thinking, Audrey? Why haven't I met him? Who is he? Who his people is?"

"That's what I want to know," Aunt Shelby gave her a thoughtful look.

Audrey held her hands up. "Y'all don't have to meet him because we aren't together anymore."

"And the jar?" Dawn asked.

Her face heated. "I haven't given it to him."

"But you prepped it, baby. That means something," Shelby said.

"I'm not talking about this," she growled.

"I guess that's all we're getting until after the full moon," Dawn said.

"You see that attitude?" Lauren asked, snickering.

"We are talking about this," Kit insisted. "Audrey, how could you hide something like this from me? How long have you been married?"

"Oop," Ness said, still clearly feeling some type of way about not being told.

Audrey growled and sent her cousin a scathing look. "Get over it, Vanessa."

"Nah, boo boo, tell Auntie Kit how long you been married," Ness shot back.

"Not now, mama. Not when my cat is so close to the surface." Her eyes pleaded with her mother.

"I want to know!" Kit snapped.

Audrey used her cat as an excuse as though all six of the other women in the room weren't also battling with their animals. Tension filled the room until it was hard to breathe. Even Eli was on edge at her back.

"Mama," she whispered, breathing deep to push down on her animal.

"Audrey." Kit was hurt. It was evident all over her face.

"Four years," she said softly.

"Oh, shit. That's..." Dawn said. "That requires wine."

"Don't you dare," Ness told her mother.

Dawn sighed but didn't move.

"You..." Kit's eyes watered. "That's a long time, Audrey. Why didn't you tell me?"

Audrey scrubbed her hand down her face and faced the truth that she'd been tap dancing around. "If I kept it to myself, then it wasn't real, and the curse couldn't touch it."

"Oh, baby," Shelby said softly.

"Audrey," Ness whispered, walking up to her. "I'm sorry for being a bitch about it."

Ness hugged her tightly. Audrey felt her cousin's remorse and was relieved. She hated being at odds with her.

Kit wiped the tears coursing down her cheeks and cleared her throat. "I'll start dinner."

"Mama," Audrey called after her.

"I understand, Audrey. We all deal with this curse in our own way. I'm hurt you didn't feel like you could talk to me about it, but I understand my part in our relationship." Kit turned her back to Audrey and started putting away groceries.

Her mother's alcoholism had colored their relationship for so long. For several years of her growing up, Audrey couldn't depend on Kit. They had worked hard when she'd become an adult to try and repair the rift from her childhood.

Audrey felt awful for keeping this secret.

Her eyes scanned the room, and there was no judgment. As Kit said, they'd each battled the curse in their separate ways. If any group of people in the world understood what she'd been going through, it was these women. She felt like shit that she'd hid her turmoil from them when she should've been leaning on them.

"I'm sorry," she said softly.

Nic grabbed her hand and squeezed.

"I want details," Lauren said, smiling to lighten the mood. She wiped her eyes and squeezed her sister's shoulder in empathy. "Is he fine?"

"So fine," Ness answered, stepping back from Audrey. "that's probably why she was really hiding him."

Aunt Dawn snickered. And just like that, the tension in the kitchen dissipated. Audrey took a deep breath and wiped a hand down her face. She would still have to talk to her mother; there would be no escaping that. But, at least the specter of her secret wasn't hanging over her head any longer.

Chapter Ten

Israel kicked his feet up on the railing and lit his blunt. He was sitting on the balcony outside of his hotel room. He could blame that habit on Eli. The kid had shown up at the exclusive private school Israel attended, a fish out of water. A scholarship kid with a chip on his shoulder that matched the size of Israel's. That had bonded them tighter than their current 'warlock with his familiar relationship' ever could. He and the lion had stayed in trouble together, or at least the school would try. Eli was the one who'd given Israel the name Lucky.

He leaned back in his chair and blew smoke up in the air. He manipulated it with his magic, molding it into the shape of a petite curvy woman. She stayed on his mind. He dissipated the smoke, and it was then that he realized the moon was full. The full moon meant that his wife was out in her cat form. He laughed and ashed his blunt.

"Oh, this is just too good."

He stood and leaned against the rail. He closed his eyes and sent his magic out into the night. The power of the town washed through him, and he shuddered. It wasn't just the Fouche Land. The whole city was inundated with old powerful magic. It was no wonder so many practitioners got in trouble here. It would've been easy to get drunk off that power and reach for things one shouldn't. He sensed all the cat shifters on the outskirts of the Taylor territory. If he wanted, Israel could take control of those cats, but they weren't what he wanted. He bypassed them. Audrey would never leave Taylor land.

He focused specifically on her magic signature. It was one he was well acquainted with. He used the connection he already had with her and targeted his magic. He smiled when he found her. He could sense her family around her; their power was tempting. He could well understand the draw for his grandmother. He used his power to push into Audrey's cat's mind. It took considerable strength. He was sweating by the time he convinced the cat to allow him entrance.

"Come to me, kitten," he said aloud, using his magic to call her closer.

Satisfied that his hold over her would ensure her compliance, he put on shoes and headed for the beach. He smiled when she ran up in her puma form twenty minutes later. She was beautiful, sleek, and slightly bigger than a natural puma. He nodded to Eli, who ran next to her in his lion form. There were other animals out running. He would guess they were shifters passing through town since they hung around the hotel beach. He ignored them and focused on his wife.

Audrey's cat came directly to him as he'd ordered. He touched their minds and reacquainted the cat with his power and touch. She took off, running along the water, and he walked behind, allowing her cat the freedom it needed. Eli and his security weren't far from them, so he didn't worry.

They spent the night together, her cat spending equal time exploring the beach and marking him with her scent. Soon though, the moon started to wan. It was almost time for her to shift back. He called her back to him, and again it took convincing for the stubborn creature to obey. He stooped down onto his haunches, running his hand across her head as she nuzzled against his leg.

"We'll get her there," he promised the puma, feeling its frustration at the distance between him and Audrey.

Her power swelled as her body started its shift. He whispered a quick spell, disguising them with his magic as she completed the change. He sat down on the cold sand, holding her close to his chest, and wrapping a blanket around her. She was asleep in his arms and would be out until morning.

It had taken a year before Audrey allowed him to be around when she shifted and another after that before her cat allowed him close to her. Israel took hope in the fact that her cat still trusted him with them. With her in his lap, he sat outside for as long as the weather allowed, happy to simply feel her curves against him.

After an hour, even with the blankets he'd conjured, it was too cold. Lifting her, he carried her up to his room. He used a washcloth to wipe her down, sliding one of his t-shirts onto her. He got her situated on her bed, getting in behind her. His body relaxed, truly relaxed for the first time in a year.

He forced himself awake way earlier than he wanted, just so that he'd get a little more time with her. He was well rested despite the small amount of hours he'd slept, and he knew it was because she was in his bed with him. He would savor the feeling, especially since it would be limited. Because the moment she awakened, she would go back to hating him. That hurt, but he was nothing if not practical, and he was reaping what he'd sowed. Not that he'd had a choice, but all the same, he couldn't blame her.

He wondered how their relationship would've evolved if he'd met her without his grandmother's interference. He traced his finger across her face, his heart aching at her beauty. She was at her most vulnerable after a shift. No artifice, no makeup, nothing was hiding her from him. He slid his thumb over her bottom lip. If it were the only time he'd get with her...he couldn't resist. He placed his lips against hers gently. Her eyes popped open when he leaned back. Emotions raced across her face so quickly. It was always the same in the morning. It was as if she woke ready to have to fight if needed.

He braced himself for her reaction. Her dark orbs met his, and his breathing stopped at the full power of her gaze. Her magic caressed his, and her unguarded thoughts were memories of the mornings they'd awaken together like this. Had he ruined what was between them? She cupped his cheek. The sadness in her eyes gutted him.

"Why, Lucky?" she whispered.

"I can't live without you, Audrey. I don't know any other way to tell you."

Her gaze caressed his face. She traced her thumb under his eyes, and he knew the exhaustion showed all over his face.

"You're not taking care of yourself." She gently admonished.

He closed his eyes and nuzzled against her hand. "That's your job, kitty cat."

She snorted. "I don't know how many times I've told you and Eli to quit calling me that."

"Give me a kiss," he ordered.

Perhaps he should've requested nicely. The possessiveness beating through his system wouldn't allow for nice. Besides, his wife knew better than anyone how he was. She leaned forward and kissed him. Her soft lips caressed his. He grabbed the back of her nape, holding her in place.

"A real kiss, kitten." He whispered against her lips.

Her eyes watered, but she obeyed, opening her mouth to him. His grip on her neck tightened as he deepened their kiss. He kept himself as restrained as he could, lazily tangling his tongue with hers when he really wanted to devour her. She pulled back and rested her forehead against his.

· · ·

Audrey took a deep breath and concentrated on putting a barrier up over her mind. Being in his presence was too tempting. Kissing him had been a bad idea. She pulled back and looked around. She'd gone out with the Taylors last night, so she well expected to be at her grandmother's house. He tensed, but she momentarily ignored him as she tried to figure out where her cat had landed her. Had Israel called her cat to him or had the damned animal sought him out?

That was a question for later.

Right now, she needed to make sure he hadn't taken her out of the state. Her eyes landed on the generic tv stand and curtains, and she relaxed marginally. She turned her gaze back to him, and her breath caught. He was so damn fine, it hurt. The asshole. His dark eyes met hers, and even though she could tell he was assessing her, his emotions were closed off to her. She couldn't be upset since she'd shut him out of her mind.

"What are you doing, Lucky?"

He lifted his hand and slid it across her short hair. "I like your hair like this," he said instead of answering.

She sighed and rolled away from him. Same shit, new day. She looked down at the t-shirt she wore. Her clothes were miles away at her house, and of course, she had no cellphone. He grabbed her as she was trying to get out of bed.

"Wait, Audrey, please."

"You don't want me, Israel. Why are you playing this game with me?" She swung her feet around and sat on the edge.

He scrambled from his side and walked over to her. "There's no way you think I don't want you."

She warmed. "Fine, you want to fuck me. That doesn't warrant a five hundred mile trip."

He kneeled in front of her, cupping her cheek. "Quit reducing what we have to sex. I wouldn't have married you just for sex."

"Right. You married me for my power." She slapped his hand away from her face and stood.

He stood and turned her to face him. "What do you need to hear from me?"

"I don't know that anything you say will help. I don't trust you with all the parts of me. Without that, this is just..." she waved her hands between them.

"I'm here, playing nice. Surely that counts for something?"

She scoffed. "Right...playing." She debated how she would get home.

She could call the house from the hotel and have someone come pick her up. That meant questions she wasn't in the mood to answer, but really, she didn't have a choice. She walked over to the desk and picked up the phone.

He sighed and ran his hand over the top of his hair. "I have way too many enemies to allow you from under my protection."

Audrey heard the whoosh of the blanket as it left the bed and wrapped around her. It pinned her hands at her side and all the anger she'd been suppressing bubbled to the surface. He had some damn nerve.

"Allow?" She snapped.

She used her magic, disintegrated the blanket wrapped around her, and flung a suspension spell at him as he tried to close the distance between them. He easily deflected it, which pissed her off even more. She growled in aggravation. She had a point to prove.

"In all the time we've been together, you could've taught me to use my magic, but you didn't. You don't want me able to protect myself. Not from your enemies, and especially not from you. It would make it much harder to access my magic, right?"

She flung another spell at him. He couldn't block all the magic sent his way. He flinched as some of it hit its mark, pinning his arms at his side.

"But while you've been hunting me down, I've been learning." The next spell got through his deflection since he couldn't raise his arms and pushed him back from her. "So I don't need your protection," she said triumphantly.

His face hardened as he broke through her spell, lifting his hands and shooting magic toward her. She quickly pushed it aside, blocking it. She didn't want to know what it would've done to her. He narrowed his eyes, and his hands moved rapidly, his mouth muttering as he gathered more magic. She didn't wait on whatever he was conjuring, pulling the coffee cups from the dresser with her power and flinging them at him. He smoothly blocked them, but it broke up the momentum of whatever spell he was doing. The sound of the breaking glass against the wall seemed to sound the ringside bell. Audrey's mind moved quickly through all the defensive spells she knew as Israel braced his feet.

They fought, throwing magic at each other and trashing the room.

"You really were teaching yourself, kitty cat. Good for you," He taunted.

She grit her teeth and bared down as a stream of his magic pressed against the shield she'd erected.

"I will have you, and I promise you, you'll enjoy every minute. Why fight me, kitten?" He lifted his hands. Audrey gasped as he flung the sheet this time towards her, wrapping her arms tight against her body.

Fuck him!

The sound of the fabric ripping satisfied her, as did the pieces of the sheet she sent to cover his face. He struggled to remove them as she dragged the office chair towards him, crashing it into his back. She laughed, and they went harder.

Israel spit feathers from his mouth as she used her power to smack him with the pillows on the bed. "Well done, kitten. You've spent our time apart well."

This time she sealed his mouth shut with the pillowcase, done with his taunting. His eyes widened in amusement as he pulled her feet from underneath her. She hit the floor and screeched in anger. He was holding back, his spells as childish as the ones she threw at him. Damn him. He moved closer with every new one he threw. She shoved wind at him, but he only stumbled slowly, his forward progress unstopping.

"I don't need you!" She gritted out, shoving a more potent spell at him as she stood to her feet.

It pushed against his shield and blew him back towards the window. He grunted as the curtains lifted, holding him in place. He snatched the curtains down and wrapped them around his body like a cape, a taunting smile on his face.

"A new look. Do you like it?" He closed the space between them faster than she could track.

"Oh, fuck you, Israel," Audrey growled and lifted her other hand.

Instead of throwing a spell, she threw a punch. He grabbed her fist before it could connect with his jaw. She was breathing hard, sweat dotting her forehead with the energy she expended. He caressed her clenched fist and unfurled her fingers. Israel kissed her fingertips as he pulled them out of a fist.

"Is this the part where I tell you that I'll change and everything between us will be okay?" he asked softly.

"Why do you push me, Israel? Just leave me be."

She had to find some kind of way to get over him. Surely she wouldn't pine for him for the rest of her life.

He lifted her hand and kissed her wrist. "I push because I can't afford to go easy on you. I have too many enemies, too many people coming after my position. I can't afford for my heart to walk around outside of my chest unprotected."

She melted. His sincerity was written all over his face. She could see it, feel it. Where his emotions had been locked down before, she realized that he'd lowered his mental shield, allowing her to see inside of him.

"That you can stand up to me, stand with me, eases me in ways you'll never understand, love." He sent the thought to her telepathically rather than speaking it aloud.

It resonated that much more because of it. A tear slipped down her cheek as her anger drained from her. She loved him, and it was something she'd been fighting since she first saw him. The whirlwind of their courtship and marriage aside, she'd fought her feelings for him, and now, he stood before her raw, and she couldn't hide it anymore.

Chapter Eleven

"Lucky."

She said his name in a way that made his dick hard. He grabbed the back of her neck and kissed her. Their tongues tangled, hot and heavy. Aggressive because of all the unresolved feelings they had between them. She stood to her toes and angled her head to kiss him deeper. He lifted her by her thighs and walked them back to a wall. She pulled back from the kiss and pulled her shirt over her head.

Even though he'd seen her naked last night, the sight of her in the daytime, willingly submitting to him...his hands shook. He didn't even know where to touch first. He cupped her cheek, bringing her body tightly into his. Heat took over, and he leaned down, dragging kisses across her chest. She moaned, and he prodded against the mental barrier she still had up. He wanted in, wanted complete access to her.

"I love looking at you," he whispered, nipping the bottom of her earlobe. He leaned over and nuzzled into her neck, dropping small kisses. "I've missed this. Missed you."

Audrey sighed in pleasure, bracing her hands on his shoulders. Israel grabbed the front of her throat and nipped her chin.

"Tell me you want me."

"I want this." She said instead.

Of course, she wouldn't easily submit to him. He didn't know what he was thinking. He removed his hand from her throat, gripped her thighs again, and lifted her. She wrapped her legs around his waist, and he carried them to the bed, bare of all its sheets. He tossed her down, and Audrey didn't move except to open her legs to him. One look at her wet and wanting had hunger overtaking all the finesse he would've typically had. He pulled her to the edge of the bed and kneeled between her legs. She gasped the moment his finger slid between the folds of her pussy. He knew of one way to make his wife submit.

The first lick reacquainted him with her taste and reminded him what he'd been missing. The second one had her back bowed as she whispered his name. She moaned and lifted her hips, gripping his hair tightly. She squirmed beneath him as he devoured her pussy, savoring her. It had only been months since they'd been apart, but he was starved for her. He sucked her clit into his mouth, inserting his fingers into her. She arched, coming apart with his name on her lips. He continued to eat her until she pushed against his head.

"I want you inside," she said breathlessly.

When he lifted from between her legs, she turned over and arched her back, giving him a daring look over her shoulder. Israel grunted and smacked her ass. Yes, he loved her in this position, but for this first time, he wanted to see her face. Look her in her eyes when he spilled inside of her. He turned her over and draped her leg over his shoulder before pushing forward. He fit his dick at her entrance, watching as it sank within her. Audrey gasped when he slid in, her eyes snapping closed.

"Unh-unh, kitten, I want to see those pretty eyes."

They popped open, and she gave him a seductive smile. He wanted this time with her to be slow and sensual as they re-familiarized themselves with each other's bodies. But, the moment he bottomed out and her scorching walls clamped down onto him, he was done. He pulled out and slammed back in, closing his eyes as ecstasy threatened to steal his control.

He caressed her leg, pushing it forward to give him more room. He drove into her, her whimpers spurring him.

"Just like that," he murmured as she met his every stroke.

"More," she panted, gripping his shoulders.

She lifted her hips, taking all of him, her nails scraping down his arms as she held on tight. He held down her hips as he fucked her, losing himself in every stroke. His magic surrounded them, reaching out to her. Israel leaned down and kissed her, his tongue mimicking the strokes of his dick, loving the slide of her skin against his. He probed her mind, frustrated that her shields were still keeping him out. He picked up his rhythm, driving harder.

"You take my dick so well," he murmured in her ear.

"Israel," she whispered, canting her hips into his.

He reached between them and thrummed her clit, kissing her, swallowing her scream as she came around him. Her pulsing center sent him over the edge, and he closed his eyes as he emptied himself in her. It was then he realized that he hadn't worn a condom. He wanted to be concerned, but he was drunk off of Audrey. He could only hope she was still on her birth control.

She hummed in satisfaction.

"Tell me I can have you again," he demanded, refusing to slide out.

He wanted to enjoy every second that he could get. Audrey wiggled her hips and ran her fingers through his beard.

"I don't have anywhere to be today."

"Say less," he whispered, devouring her mouth.

Israel clutched Audrey closer, pulling her legs between his, so they were tightly pressed together. He was exhausted. They'd gone at it for hours, including this last time in the shower, before he finally slipped into bed with her. Now, she smelled of his soap, and he got a possessive thrill from that. Her soft skin glided across his as she slid her leg along his. Her hands traced patterns along his stomach as her breath brushed across his chest.

In the years they were together, it had always been like this. She would come to him and stay. They'd fuck every chance they got until something spooked her, and she left. She claimed work, checking on her mother, anything to put distance between them. It had fit his purposes at first. He used her absences to stall his grandmother. But a year ago, he'd finally confessed to his grandmother that he had no intentions of carrying out her plan. He should've known she'd taken it too easy. Annabelle had purposely sought Audrey out to tell her what he'd done, sending her packing.

His grandmother couldn't have come up with a better punishment, really.

He'd missed Audrey every day they'd been separated.

"We can't keep doing this, Lucky."

He sighed because she was right. "But you're the one doing all the running, love."

She lifted her face to meet his gaze. "You're right."

"Why?" It was the question he wanted above all. He could convince her to come back to him. She always did. But, this time, he needed to know why, so he could finally convince her to stay.

"I'm working on the why."

"And we can be together while you work on it?" He nuzzled into her neck.

She sighed and tangled her fingers in his hair. "I don't want anything bad to happen to you while I do."

He frowned and pulled back. "Audrey, my lifestyle is dangerous. I'm aware of that and move accordingly. It's not your place to worry about that."

She snorted. "I'm your wife; it's absolutely my place. But, all that aside, being with me puts you in more danger. But, I'm going to fix it."

He searched her face and realized she was serious and wouldn't budge. "I'm not letting you go."

"Just for a little while," she murmured, kissing his lips.

"Let me help you with whatever it is."

She studied him. "We'll see."

That answer was noncommittal, and it irritated him. She cupped his cheek and kissed him, and just like that, his thoughts strayed to more pleasurable subjects. In the back of his mind, though, were plans. He didn't care how long it took. He would gain his wife's trust.

Chapter Twelve

udrey cursed as her name was called yet again. This time louder. She'd hardly gotten any sleep. She'd finally convinced Israel to let her go somewhere around three this morning, and she had plans to spend the morning sleeping after the marathon of sex they'd had. Her body was achy and sore in places that brought a reluctant smile to her face. She gave up burrowing under the blankets and threw them from over her head.

"What!"

Her mother raised an eyebrow. "I'll pretend like you ain't talking to me like that. Get up and wear something you can be outside in."

Kit left the room confident that her daughter had no plans to ignore her order. She was right, which made Audrey all the more irritated as she brushed her teeth and washed her face. She trudged down the stairs in a pair of jeans, and a long sleeve shirt, her hiking books dangled from her fingers. She frowned at the kitchen full of her aunts. Nic and Ness both shot her alarmed looks before shrugging.

"It's barely six o'clock. Where in the world are we going?" Audrey didn't address her question to any one person. She didn't care who answered.

"I owe you girls an explanation from the other day," was Kit's answer.

They all piled into her Aunt Shelby's minivan and got on the road. Her curiosity truly peaked when they pulled off to the side of the road only minutes later. They pulled off the road and into the woods.

"We walk from here."

Audrey frowned and met Nic's glance. They knew this area. It was where her grandmother's hidden garden was. Instead of going in the way that JT showed them, the aunts went in a different direction. Now she was bewildered, especially when they came out into the clearing with the flowers.

"You went in a different way," Nic said with a frown, turning in a circle.

"So you do know about these plants?" Kit stated.

Nic nodded. "JT brought me here. Grandmother was selling some of these."

The women shared a look.

"We planted these originally." Kit admitted.

Audrey's mouth dropped open. "So you know what they do?"

She had been experimenting with the ones Nic told her were safe to use. They only used the ones her grandmother had been selling, leaving the others for Nicole to research more.

Kit wiped a hand down her face. "They are different species of what we call the Andisa plant. I don't know what anyone else calls it."

Dawn touched her sister's shoulder. "These flowers can amplify power."

"What kind of power?" Audrey asked, getting excited.

"Any kind of power. It depends on the plant." Kit sighed and looked around and pointed at violet glowing one. "That one amplifies the connection to the other side of the veil. That one," indicating a sickly yellow one, "amplifies poisons, curses. And that red one," she took a deep breath, and tears crested her eyes. "That one amplifies the power put into a spell."

Audrey stepped closer to her mother.

Kit put a hand up. "I planted the yellow one to see if it would work. The plant is rare and was damn near extinct. It took me and Will Taylor years to procure it. Once that one worked, I begged Lauren to help me propagate the seeds for the violet and red ones. Dawn helped me with some spells to test them. The last one... We'd just lost your father, and I couldn't...I couldn't let him go. I combined them, thinking I could access his soul on the other side. I found...Oh god..." She whispered and walked away, tears pouring down her face.

Dawn was crying, and Lauren and Shelby's faces were resolute.

"She found someone drug addicted. He was out of it, unaware of what was happening. Kit was going to use his body." Dawn admitted.

Audrey felt sick.

Ness frowned. "You were using necromancy?"

"It was a form of it, yes. I was going to give David a new body, but it would still be him." Kit confessed.

"Mom," Audrey whispered, horrified.

"It backfired," Lauren said with a tired sigh. "Kit asked Dawn to help, and not only did it not work, but the backlash...." Lauren covered her eyes.

"Magic always requires a price, dark magic more so. It took mama years to reverse what we had done," Dawn said.

"So those years where you were both on drugs and alcohol had nothing to do with the curse?" Ness asked.

Kit shook her head, her eyes pleading for Audrey to understand.

"Is my father at peace?" She whispered. It was the only thing she cared to know.

"Lauren and I sent him back," Shelby assured her.

"So, you knew he was in some kind of 'thrall' while alive, and your solution was to bring him back to life under the same conditions. Am I getting that right?" Audrey snapped.

"No, Audrey, I thought—"

She cut her mother off. "It sounds like you selfishly wanted him back, no matter his quality of life."

Audrey walked away from them all, trekking back to the van. She couldn't...on top of everything else in her life. She couldn't deal with it. She'd done her damndest to learn her magic on the off chance she'd end up like her mother and to find out now that magic was the reason for her mother's drug problem. And Israel wanted this...this tainted magic? She couldn't fathom it. It had her second-guessing all the things she'd done to boost her own magic. Would she end up like her mother and Israel in her search for more power?

He could still smell Audrey in the room. He sat at the desk chair and stared at the rumpled bed. The memories from their sex this morning had him hard as hell and frustrated to boot. He reluctantly let her go back to her grandmother's house in the wee hours of the morning. He even went so far as to call off Eli. He was still second-guessing that decision. Israel looked up at the knock on his door. The beep of the lock disengaging sounded next. He eyed his best friend as he walked in. Something was obviously wrong because Eli's face was somber.

Eli's eyes widened as he took in the state of the room. "The fuck happen here?"

"Audrey."

Eli smiled and looked around. "I told you not to play with that girl. I still can't believe you called off her detail."

Israel shrugged. After the display this morning, he felt a little better about it. "For now. Why are you here?"

"Your grandmother is on her estate."

Israel frowned and reconsidered sending Eli back to Audrey. "How long?"

"Maybe a week, far as I can tell," Eli answered.

He sighed and just shook his head. She'd been in town as long as he had. What was one more thing on his plate? He knew one person he could call to find out what was happening with his grandmother.

"Keep me posted if you hear anything else."

Eli nodded. "Will do."

He waited until his friend left the room before he pulled out his cellphone. He video called his aunt and waited while the other end rang. He was surprised when his little sister's face popped up. Happiness flooded him as it did any time he talked to Arianne. But, she was supposed to be at the boarding school his grandmother paid ridiculous amounts of his money for her to attend.

"Riri," he greeted her.

"Lucky! I miss you!"

"I miss you too, love. Why aren't you in school?"

She gave him a sheepish smile. "Grandmother pulled me out for a couple of weeks."

His stomach fluttered, and nervous energy flooded his body. "Did she say why?"

"Some kind of family event." His sister shrugged, unconcerned. "Why are you calling TiTi Sabine's phone and not mine?"

"I assumed you would be in class. Plus, I need to talk to TiTi," he told her.

Arianne looked off to the side and gave who he assumed was their aunt a mischievous smile. "Fine, call me later."

"I will. Love you."

"I love you more," she told him.

Sabine's beautiful face filled the phone. His aunt was in her late fifties, yet her mocha brown skin was unlined and unblemished. As the youngest Deleon sister, she'd been pampered her entire life, which showed in how well she cared for herself. Right now, her carefully dyed hair was jet black and pulled back from her narrow face into a low bun. The white dress shirt she wore was opened to the top of her collarbone, and the tasteful gold jewelry she wore showcased her casual wealth. Her makeup was minimal, though she never went without it. Appearances meant a lot to his family, and though Sabine fought her mother on most things, she adhered strictly to that.

"TiTi."

She eyed him. "I take it you've heard, then."

"Just now," he informed her. "What is she up to?"

Sabine sighed and nervously fiddled with the thin Cuban link necklace around her neck. "Mother was approached by the history museum to do an exhibit for Black History Month."

He scoffed. "And she agreed?"

"Mother is vain above all things. She'll take any opportunity to remind the people in this area how far the Deleon's go back. There's going to be a huge gala around it and a few of the other major families here."

"Is that why she pulled Arianne out of school?"

He could see the background shift around Sabine as she walked away; he was assuming for more privacy.

"I gather you've pissed her off in some manner?"

"She wants my wife."

Sabine frowned. "You told her no." It wasn't posed as a question.

"I'm not draining Audrey. Do you think I want Grandmother more powerful than she already is?"

"You don't have to tell me, Israel." She pinched the bridge of her nose. "Last's month's ceremony wasn't up to her standards?"

He grunted.

"You can't keep this up, my love." She said softly.

"I renewed the covenant, TiTi. You know the consequences."

"I wish you had listened to me."

"Would you rather my little sister had gone through the ceremony? If she had survived, can you imagine her doing what I do monthly for this family?"

Sabine sighed, her eyes showcasing her tumultuous emotions. "This family will use you until there is nothing left. I worry for you, Israel."

"Until Arianne is powerful enough to fend for herself, there is no escape for me. For now, feeding power to this family and the goddess will continue."

He didn't like it any more than his aunt did. The power exchanges he performed every month for the covenant's sake were eating at his conscious—what was left of it. But if he had to do it again, he would gladly take his little sister's place.

Sabine studied him through the phone before finally giving up the argument with a shake of her head. "Don't worry. I'm keeping Arianne glued to my side." She assured him.

"Thank you, Titi." He shook his head and changed the subject. "What is this exhibit supposed to be?"

"The curator is asking for pictures, books, anything we have that will show the family's history. Mother has been combing the estate for the past week."

"Is she donating them to the museum, or are they only for display the night of the gala?"

He thought back to the conversation he had with Audrey last night. She was worried about him, and he had an idea why. She'd declined his help, but...there was something he could do.

"TiTi, can you make sure Grandfather's almanac is in that collection?"

Sabine studied him. "What are you up to, Lucky?"

"It won't fall back on you or Arianne, I swear."

She sighed. "Fine, anything else?"

He wanted to be greedy and ask for more of his grandfather's things. When he'd left the house years ago, all he'd been able to take was the journal he'd been reading at the time and some of his father's books. He longed to go back to the estate and grab all of his father's things, but it was one more thing Annabelle held over his head. He would hold off, though, because what he was going to attempt was risky as it was.

"When is the Gala?"

"I'll send you an invite if Mother hasn't already. You'll be expected to be here in full regalia."

He nodded, shifting some things around in his head to pull his plan off. "Thank you, Titi Sabine."

"Of course, my love. Anything for you."

He hung up, satisfied that he had a plan in place now, if he could convince his wife to allow him to help.

It could be the thing that finally glued her to his side.

Chapter Thirteen

Doing spellwork with her head all over the place was never a good idea. But, working on spells, especially complicated ones, was something Audrey found relaxing. It was just one more thing she'd found out about herself since moving to Georgia. So much of her life had been spent ignoring the magic that was a part of her family. Until yesterday, she thought it was why her mother and Aunt Dawn had hidden in their vices. Her mind was still reeling from finding out that it had been the result of dabbling in dark magic.

Her gaze strayed over to the red andisa plant. Her mother said it amplified spells, and Audrey had confirmed it by reading her grandmother's journal. She was worried a little about using it, but according to Patsy's journal, the kickback should be fine if used in small quantities.

It brought her mind back to Kit and what she'd done. Her mother had played with magic she hadn't been able to handle. Could the same thing happen to her and Aunt Shelby for attempting this spell? Her mother's gift for spells was the same as Audrey's, and if Kit couldn't handle the power from the andisa, could she?

"You sure you want to do this now, Audrey?" Aunt Shelby's voice was soft...gentle. As though she were afraid of spooking her.

She sighed and completed the circle she was setting up around her aunt. "Doing spells calms me."

"I'm interested to see if it works," Nicole spoke up from the door.

She and Ness watched from the doorway to give her space to work. They also were on standby in case something went wrong. Audrey took a deep breath and worked to stifle all her wayward thoughts. This spell was a first for her, and she didn't want to harm her aunt with carelessness.

Aunt Shelby smiled at her. "You're fine. We double and triple-checked that spell."

Audrey finished drawing the circle and sat on the inside, across from her aunt. Part of Audrey's power was seeing the inner workings of spells. She'd asked her aunt Shelby to sit with her so she could examine her. Aunt Shelby had the curse affect her first hand. She could've asked her mother, but she was lowkey still disappointed in her.

"I don't want to fuck up the flow of your chi, TiTi."

She smiled at her. "Honey, trust me. I been at it a long time. I'm not worried."

Audrey nodded. "Okay, then, here goes nothing."

She closed her eyes and clutched the crystal in her hand tightly. She pulled on the power she'd been learning to wield. When she opened her eyes, her aunt was wide open to her. Shelby's thoughts were steady, concentrating solely on leaving herself open enough for Audrey to use her. Audrey took a moment to marvel at the amount of power swirling around Aunt Shelby. She moved from Shelby's thoughts and focused on her aunt's chakras. All seven were strong, though her crown chakra was lit brighter than the others. The waves of her aunt's power flowed around these chakras, a river of motion. Audrey saw the dark spot in the middle of her heart chakra. This would be the tricky part.

Audrey quietly chanted the spell they'd prepared and held the crystal in her hand like a dagger. Once she finished, the crystal in her hand warmed, and she directed it, touching that dark spot. She placed the spell, and like a stone in a flowing river, Shelby's chakra waves moved around the crystal point, allowing Audrey a peek past that dark area. Like pulling open curtains, the cause of the dark spot was revealed.

Audrey studied the dark magic that composed the curse. It was weaved into her aunt's DNA, marking it as a generational curse. She could see the makings of it but not quite how it had been put together. Squinting her eyes, she gasped. The signature left behind on the curse was familiar. She'd tasted that magic just yesterday.

After a few more minutes of examining the curse, she pulled back, frustrated. She sighed and pulled her magic back.

"What did you see?" Ness asked.

"I saw the components of the curse," she muttered, shaking her head to clear her thoughts. She thought about the familiar feel of the dark magic. "What's the name of the family that cursed us? The Surname?"

"Deleon," Shelby answered.

Audrey's heart clenched. "That's Israel's family."

"Well, shit," Nic said.

Shelby held up her hand. "Putting that aside for later, what did you see?"

Audrey rubbed her forehead. "So, I can see the spell and the individual parts of it, but I don't think I can replicate it."

"But you have all the parts," Nic said.

"Yeah, but spellwork is like a gumbo," Shelby said. "Everyone can have the recipe, but everyone also has their way of making it different. Their own family secret ingredient, the way they prep the roux, all of that counts and can make an entirely different tasting dish."

Audrey nodded, feeling discouraged.

Ness gripped her shoulder. "Don't do that. We have the pieces. We can go from there."

"I need to go to Israel," she told them.

Her cousins give her a shocked look.

"It's his family. I know he doesn't deal with them, but he may be able to get us the exact 'recipe.'"

They all gave her a look she couldn't quite decipher.

"Do you think he'll help you?" Nic asked.

"He wants me. I can use that for leverage."

"Not you finna whore yourself out, chile," Ness drawled.

Her cheeks burned, and the rest of her body heated, not in embarrassment but in want. She and Israel had never had issues in the bedroom, and the other day had been no exception. She shuddered, thinking about his weight on top of her. He was so aggressive in bed, in all the best ways. Yeah...it would be no hardship to seduce her husband.

Nic snickered, and Aunt Shelby shot them chastising looks. "This is serious, Audrey. I've felt his power around town. He's very powerful."

"I can do it." She assured her aunt.

More to the point, she wanted to do it.

"And this has nothing to do with him dicking you down the other night?" Ness asked.

Nic cackled. "She talking about saving the family when really she wants to go back for round two. You ain't gotta lie to kick it, cuz."

The girls laughed. Even Aunt Shelby tucked her lips to hide her smirk.

"All y'all hot in the ass. Help me up," Shelby demanded.

Audrey stood and helped her aunt up. "I trust you know what you're doing. He's your husband, so you know better than us."

Audrey nodded, and Shelby left.

She turned to her cousins, and they were both smiling at her.

"Want us to help you pick out a freak'em dress?" Nic asked.

"Bump you both," Audrey said, hiding her smile. She sobered. "We have a chance at breaking this curse. How can I not take it?"

Ness grabbed her hand and gripped it tight. "We're together in this, so whatever you need from us."

Nic echoed the sentiment. "As long as you think it's safe, then we're behind you."

Audrey nodded and went to shower. She had a husband to lure.

Chapter Fourteen

Israel stared at the envelope sitting on the desk. Anger coursed through him, along with wariness. The envelope itself was innocuous. Heavy stock paper, elegant calligraphy spelling out his full government name. Nothing out of the ordinary.

He'd been eager to answer the door, expecting his wife to be on the other side. He'd thought nothing of the hotel employee passing along the envelope. It wasn't until he'd opened it and the letter from his grandmother slid out that he'd gotten pissed. Having talked to his aunt, he knew the invitation had been forthcoming.

He hadn't expected it to come to his hotel room.

His grandmother's words hadn't been threatening exactly. The summons was simple and to the point. But knowing his sister was home, under the thumb of Annabelle, made every saccharine sentence an underlying threat. Her simply knowing exactly where to find him wasn't something he was worried about, he could take care of himself, but Arianne was vulnerable, thus making his attendance a demand, not a request. He was already planning to attend the gala, but impotent fury filled him. Israel cursed and danced flames over Annabelle's letter, watching it burn to ash. He swiped his hands, dissipating the ashes, and scanned the invitation to make sure nothing of his grandmother lingered. She was a clever magic wielder, and he wouldn't put it past her to spy on him.

Finding no trace of magic, he relaxed his shoulders, his mind spinning. He'd devised a tentative plan to help his wife, and with every new act from his grandmother, he realized how challenging the task would be. Of course, if Audrey would let him help, the whole thing would go easier, but it seemed she was stubborn and back to her old ways. He thought they were in a good place when she'd left his room a couple of days ago, but she hadn't answered his calls, mentally or by telephone. He had an idea of what was holding her back, hence the current plan he was working on. He knew the stakes were high, and his grandmother had raised them by bringing Arianne home.

Of all his enemies, the women in his life stressed him out the most.

A knock at his door brought him out of his thoughts. He tensed. Now that Annabelle knew where he was, he'd be wary and on guard of every little thing. He sucked in a surprised breath when he opened the door. Audrey was on the other side and dressed to entice. The black leather skirt she wore reached her knees, but a split, lined with gold buttons, was open all the way to the top of her thigh. The camel trench coat she wore was draped across her shoulders, revealing the plunging black top. He swallowed hard, his eyes devouring her. The heels she wore made her legs look long, lean, and perfect.

She smiled coyly and slid past him. "Can I come in?"

His eyes followed her, widening when she slid the coat from her shoulders. Lord have mercy, there was no back to the top she wore. Of course, his body reacted immediately. It was hers to control, always had been. He was helpless where she was concerned. She'd done this their entire marriage, run when she got scared of her feelings, but she'd always come back to him, seducing his body and wooing him with her affection.

"Why haven't you been answering my calls?" He was finally able to ask.

"Family stuff."

He swallowed a frustrated growl. It was the same story she'd always given him when she ran. He took her back every time, enjoying any time he could get with her. At first, it hadn't bothered him. She'd been a means to an end, and he didn't necessarily want or need her up under him. But then, she'd stayed almost a year that last time, and he'd grown attached to her. When she left seven months ago and didn't return, he cycled through worry, fury, and betrayal. Even though it had only been days this time, those same feelings were bubbling inside.

"And why are you here now, after ignoring me for two days?"

She sauntered closer, weaving her hands behind his neck. "You're my husband. Do you not want me, Lucky?"

Her use of his nickname softened him. He rested his forehead against hers. "Truth, kitten," He demanded.

He would take her any way she was willing to give herself to him, but he wanted...no needed the truth of why. It would help him manage his expectations.

She cupped his chin and brought him close for a kiss. He gave in to her, devouring her mouth. He gripped her ass and pulled her tightly to him.

'I've missed you,' he said it telepathically. Really, it slipped out, the desperate tone surprising even him.

Audrey stiffened and backed up, her chest rising and falling with her harsh breathing. "Iz." She sighed. "I thought I could do this...but I can't. I'm not built like you."

He flinched; he felt the condemnation in that. "What do you want from me, Audrey? You only have to tell me."

Her eyes flashed, her cat lashing across their connection. "Don't do that."

"Do what?"

"Do that soothing tone as though you're being reasonable, and I'm the one who won't cooperate."

"I..." what the hell did he say to that?

She ran a hand over the top of her hair. It was colored again, this time a lavender color that fit her face just as well as the red had earlier.

She took a deep breath. "I need your help."

"Anything," he quickly promised.

"Your family cursed mine."

He fought to keep his face neutral. He'd hoped she wouldn't find out. Unfortunately, Audrey could read him like no one else.

"You knew."

He held up his hand to stall the cursing out he knew was coming. "It's a part of why I sought you out."

"What the fuck is your family's problem?" She snapped. "It wasn't enough that they put a generational curse on our family. You had to circle back to inflict extra torture."

"I had no intention of helping my grandmother." He hastened to explain.

"But you sought me out. You waited until I was at my most vulnerable, and you took advantage of that. What was the reason?"

He decided to come clean. They couldn't move without it. He clenched his hands, his whole body tensing as he realized what he'd have to tell his wife. It would leave him raw, open...but how could he ask her to trust him if he were unwilling to do the same. His eyes traced her face, the words trapped behind his fear of her reaction. She waited patiently for him to speak, but he could feel her probing at his mind for the answers herself.

"My grandmother pointed you out to me, and you stole my breath, Audrey. Yes, I played along, but I never had any intentions of stealing your power...." He took a deep breath... "not when I could harness it for myself," he finished quietly.

She was stock still, her shock blanketing him. He stepped forward, but she held up a hand and stepped back.

"All of it. I want all of the truth," she whispered.

He swallowed the lump in his throat. "My family doesn't have innate power the ways yours does, but we are experts in wielding arcane magic. We have a spell we've used for centuries. It transfers innate magic to us for our use. That's my job in the family. I'm the one responsible for bringing in new power. Annabelle wanted yours. She gets a kick out of finding Fouche's, no matter how distant, and taking their power. I...I had no plans to steal your power, but being married to you, tied to you, would give me access to it. Do you understand how much more powerful I would be with access to your magic? I rule Miami, but I could rule all of Florida with it."

"Oh God," she whispered. "It's never been about me. In the four years, you have never cared an ounce for me. All this time, I've been leaving to spare you to, to save you." Her eyes watered, and it broke his heart.

"Audrey," he whispered.

She took another step back. "Don't you dare touch me."

"It's different now." He swore.

"Liar," She hissed. "You came all the way up here with the same damn games."

He nodded. "I admit that. But seeing you here, seeing how your family makes your whole being light up changed that."

"I don't believe you."

That was fair, and he didn't blame her.

"I need time."

She walked out the door without looking back, and Israel lashed out, slinging magic, first breaking the desk where his laptop was, then the chair. He was breathing hard. Eli rushed into the room.

Eli eyed the destroyed furniture. "Lucky?"

He held up his hand. "I'm good."

Eli studied him a moment more. "Talk to me, Iz. What's good?"

"I fucked up," was all he could say.

"Maybe this one thing you fucked up, but nothing is saying you can't fix it," Eli told him softly.

He shook his head. Deep in his heart, the look on her face when she left...if she came back, he knew it would never be the same.

Chapter Fifteen

The pressure on her chest was making it hard to breathe.

Audrey fumbled at the car door, her hands shaking as she finally got it opened. She slid into the seat, her body starting to tremble as the weight of Israel's words sank into her. She'd felt his fear at having to tell her, but she'd not felt an ounce of remorse. His grandmother had told her and warned that Israel only wanted her power. But, she'd still held out hope that their time together had changed him.

She'd gone into their sham of a marriage knowing that Israel would do anything to keep rule over his city. But, she'd naively thought she wouldn't be affected by his gluttony for power. She'd carried guilt for the effect the family's curse would have on him as well as remorse for the way she'd handled it. The in and out she'd done during their marriage hadn't been the best way to deal with her fast-growing feelings for him.

But she'd done it to keep him safe.

Now to find out that he'd never been in danger for falling for her...Their marriage had been nothing to him but a game. Her heart hurt. She slammed up a dampening spell over her car and screamed until her throat was raw. Hurt and anger festered inside of her for both Israel and her mother. Just when she thought it couldn't get any worse. All the people around her were deceitful and selfish, their pursuit of magic poisonous. She laid her head on the steering wheel and sobbed. Warmth filled her, and the scent of her grandmother filled the car.

She took a shuddering breath. "I don't know if I can do this, Grandmother," she whispered. "I'm not built for this, not like Nic and Ness. Help me," she begged, tears running down her cheeks.

Her body heated, the smell got stronger, and Audrey could feel her grandmother's presence filling the car. She closed her eyes tight, savoring the feeling of Patsy. A wind blew in the car, drying her face, and a renewed sense of purpose overtook her. She would suck up her pride for the sake of the family and the love her cousin had found. At least one of them would come out of this with their heart intact.

"Thank you," she whispered and straightened in the seat.

She wiped her face for good measure and took a deep breath. She checked her makeup in the mirror and repaired it as best she could. Removing the spell, she walked back to the hotel and back up to Israel's room. Audrey nearly broke down again when he came to the door. The dark circles under his eyes told of his exhaustion. His dark eyes were dull, the resigned expression on his face threatening her resolve. She loved him so fucking much, and that was just too bad.

She cleared her throat. "I still need your help."

He stepped back and allowed her entrance. She looked around at all the destruction in the room and swallowed her questions. She refused to care.

"I need the spell your family used to curse my family."

"I don't have access to it."

She gnashed her teeth. "Then get access. In order to reverse it, I need to know how it's made."

"I'll help you do it. Whatever you need. Can we talk about—"

She cut him off. "No. Once this is done, we're done. I can't let you trample over my heart, Israel. I need it whole for the next person I give it to."

"There will be no next person," he growled, stepping closer to her. "You are mine."

"I was never yours." She left the room before she changed her mind.

She drove home on autopilot. Nic and Ness met her at the door.

Nic's concerned gaze raked over her face. "What happened?"

"He's agreed to help."

Ness stepped forward and cupped her cheek. "How can I fix it, Audrey? Whatever's wrong, tell me how to fix it." Her cousin whispered.

It broke Audrey, and the tears started. Nic and Ness enveloped her in a hug that helped. Her mother came around the corner.

"Audrey, what's wrong?" Kit asked.

"Not now, mama."

Kit stepped towards her. "We have to talk."

"I don't have anything to say to you at the moment. I'm tired."

"Audrey, you love this Israel person; surely you understand." Kit tried anyway.

"No, I don't understand. Magic is this beautiful, pure thing you and Israel would twist to your purposes. You loved my father so much that you corrupted what was inside you, and do you know what that did, mama? It left a shell that I had to deal with...that I had to clean up and baby and keep alive. You loved daddy so much that there was never any love left for me."

Kit reached for her. "No, Audrey, that's not true."

Audrey snatched her arm from her mother's reach. "It feels true!"

She shook her head and headed upstairs. She shucked off her outfit and got into bed in just her underwear, pulling the blanket over her head.

She didn't remember going to sleep, but she knew she was in a dream when she sat up. Her grandmother was sitting on the edge of her bed. Patsy was beautiful, appearing younger than she had been in real life. Her face was glowing and flush with power and contentment. She wore a pair of white linen pants with a matching shirt. It contrasted with her dark brown skin making her appear healthy and hearty.

"I felt you earlier. Thank you," Audrey told her.

"My sensitive Audrey." Patsy waved for her to come closer.

Audrey got out from under the blankets and rushed to her grandmother's side. She laid her head on Patsy's shoulder.

"All that fighting and pushing people away to protect that soft gooey center." Patsy chided, settling her cheek against the top of Audrey's hair.

"I thought he loved me," she whispered.

"It's not my place to speak on what he feels, my love."

"I can break the curse, Grandmother," Audrey told her.

"And I'm already pre-proud of you."

Audrey smiled.

"You're using the curse to hold yourself back from him."

"He was using me, he doesn't have any feelings for me, so it's a moot point."

"If you take the time to think over his words, you'll understand that that's not quite the case."

Audrey scoffed. "Did you finally visit me to advocate for a Deleon?"

Patsy chuckled. "I came to visit you because the hard part is coming."

Audrey shuddered.

"You and your cousins are stronger than your mothers, so I don't doubt your abilities. Just prepare yourself and your cousins for the fallout."

She turned and faced her grandmother. "What fallout?"

"You'll see, and you'll guide them. As much as you may not want to believe it, Israel is a part of that. The things the two of you could do together, love. If you'd only get out of your own way."

Audrey sighed, unsure what to say to that or how to reconcile her feelings with Israel and her mother had done.

"Your love for magic is a pure and beautiful thing, Audrey. Show him that. Show him another way."

She nodded, taking her grandmother's words to heart.

"I've given Nicole her purpose, and she's doing it even as we speak. I'm giving you yours. Prepare the family. You have the journals, and you're the cleverest person I've ever witnessed with a spell. I believe in you. I love you." Patsy said, cupping her cheek.

Audrey closed her eyes and reveled in the feel of that soft, cool touch she remembered. She could even smell the lavender of the lotion her grandmother kept by the kitchen sink for when she washed her hands.

"I love you, Grandmother." She said as she opened her eyes for one last look.

Patsy nodded. "Now, back to bed."

She tucked Audrey into bed and kissed her forehead as she'd done so many years before. And Audrey drifted off, feeling renewed and refreshed.

Chapter Sixteen

Israel growled at the banging door. Who the fuck was it now? He knew his security wouldn't be at his door like that, especially since he'd told them to leave him alone. Audrey had left hours ago, and he was in no mood for whatever was on the other side of the door. He opened it and was surprised to see Audrey's cousin, Nicole. She slapped him, and he stumbled back, feeling her magic behind the physical assault.

"That's for making my cousin cry. This..." she held out a candle, "is for protection."

He didn't know what to think or how to react. He stared at her extended arm for a long moment before grabbing the candle.

"And before you kill your security, it's not their fault." She pointed her thumb towards the hallway.

Curious, he stuck his head out the door and saw the new 'twins' slumped over, with JT leaning against the hallway, the wolf's arms crossed over his chest. JT wore a dazed look on his face that made Israel frown. Ignoring it for now, he leaned back into his room and eyed the petite witch. Her power danced around her, her fury in no way disguised.

"Why would I take anything from you?"

"I don't give a shit at the moment, Israel *Deleon*. But, my grandmother appointed me to keep those chosen for my cousins safe. You're it for Audrey."

He was stunned, and his heart started racing, some of the hopelessness he'd been feeling dissipating. "She said that? Audrey said that?"

Nicole didn't answer, only tilted her head to study him. "I don't know what you did, but you need to fix it, and that's as far as I will get in y'all's business. Light the candle every night for the next seven days."

With that information, she strutted off, leaving him in a daze. He could've done any manner of things to the woman for daring to put her hands on him, but he'd been too stunned. He used his power to examine the candle and frowned deeper. It was a protection spell. For him? Clearly, Nicole didn't like him. But she said she'd been appointed? It was confusing. As much as he hurt, her words circled his head, replacing the ones Audrey had given him before she'd left.

He was 'it' for Audrey.

Could he put his hope in that? She'd asked him for help breaking the curse, and since he'd already planned to do that, he needed to get to work. He rushed over to the desk and straightened it, using his magic to put back together the broken lamp. Audrey had asked for the spell itself, and while he couldn't help her with that, he could do the next best thing.

He booted up his laptop and opened a document he kept behind a password. It was the last link Israel had to his father and grandfather. It was passages from a journal he'd been given by his father a year before he died. According to his father, his grandfather and great-grandfather had kept the journal, passing it down to the next in a single line to the men that married into the family until it got to his father and then him.

Israel was supposed to be adding to the pages, documenting his life for the next after him, but from the moment he touched the book, he couldn't bring himself to add any new pages.

He had a feeling that they'd be disappointed in how he'd chosen to use his magic.

Instead of taking after them, using his power to mitigate the damage the women in his family would do, he'd joined them. He'd had no issues renewing his family's covenant and renewing their power. As far as he was concerned, he used that power just as much as they did. He'd used it to build his empire in Miami, much like they'd done in Savannah. He'd escaped from under their thumb the moment he could, forgoing the duty the men in his family claimed to have. What did he care if the Deleon women rained their power down on those around him? So long as he wasn't under their control, he couldn't care less.

At least until his mother had had his little sister.

Arianne had changed the game. Annabelle used his little sister as an insurance plan to keep him in line. They both knew he would do nothing to her when Arianne could possibly suffer for it. It was how she'd initially gotten him to renew the covenant with the goddess. Israel sighed and thought back to that day. His grandmother had called to tell him that it was time to renew the covenant and that Arianne was the only 'woman' in the family left to do it. The 'woman' in question was eight at the time. He'd been furious, but he'd known Annabelle, and she would do it regardless of the consequences to his sister. Against his better judgment, he'd volunteered himself.

He would never turn down more power.

Until he'd met Audrey, he'd had no issues sacrificing other magic users to keep his family in power. Once he met her, once he'd gotten a taste of her innocence, basked in the light that surrounded her...Israel had felt the weight of the things he'd done. He'd had no plans on telling Audrey what he did to keep power. He couldn't face the condemnation from her. And now, he'd face it anyway.

Israel shook his head and concentrated on the task ahead of him. Instead of adding to the journal, he'd digitized the records so that he could refer to them whenever he needed to without damaging the book, allowing him to keep it in a secure spot. He didn't think his grandmother knew he had the journal, but he didn't want to take any chances. Annabelle refused to deal with computers, so digitizing Jacob's journal kept it out of her hands. He pushed through the pages until he was back far enough into his great-grandfather's section. Jacob was the son of Henry—the first Deleon to initiate the curse over the Fouche's— and had documented the things his father had told him. Israel had read the passages before. It was how he'd known he could step in for his sister.

The exact spell for the curse wasn't in the journal, but...according to Jacob, there was a place where he could find a counter spell for it. Henry had made it as a just in case. Israel wondered if his great-grandfather hadn't died if he would've allowed the curse on the Fouche's to last for as long as it had.

Even as Israel tried to concentrate on the journal entries, his mind drifted back to Audrey. He didn't think she was coming back. The hurt on her face...he would see that look in his nightmares, if he got the chance to sleep. He needed to see her, to try and explain better. He stood and grabbed his jacket. Eli met him at the door, his hand poised to knock.

"Where are you going?"

"To talk to Audrey."

Eli sighed but fell in step with him. "Lucky, I thought you were going to give her space?"

"I've given her months' worth of space!" He snapped, slapping the elevator button. "This shit won't get any better if she won't talk to me."

Eli nodded but said nothing else. "Where are we going?"

He closed his eyes and felt the bond with her. It was stronger than it had been in months. He could damn near pinpoint where she was. "She's at her grandmother's house."

"Iz."

"Just drive, Eli." He ordered.

Cursing to himself, Eli followed orders. The drive over was quiet as Israel tried to find the right words to get Audrey to talk to him. With Annabelle knowing where he was, the most urgent thing to him at the moment was her safety, but somehow he didn't think that would matter to her.

His eyes widened when they got to the Fouche property line. Instead of being stopped like last time, Eli was able to drive right through. A triumphant thrill zipped through Israel. Though they could cross the boundary, he felt the magic pressing against his aura. It was a warning, and his powers dampened the closer they approached the house.

Powerful shit.

And he couldn't help the lust for it that rose.

"Stay in the car," he murmured to Eli, not wanting to make the situation any tenser.

Eli snorted and got out anyway. By the time they stepped out of the car, Nicole and Ness were both standing on the porch, arms crossed over their chests.

"What are you doing here, Deleon?" Ness asked.

"I just want to talk to Audrey." He held up his hands in a gesture of peace.

"She's resting," Nic told him.

"And we ain't passing no messages," Ness stated emphatically.

He cursed and pulled on his bond with Audrey, hoping to get her to answer. She didn't, and for a moment, he wavered.

"Ahh shit," Eli said softly next to him.

Israel sighed. He could hear them, hell, feel their power. In moments, he and Eli were surrounded by motorcycles. Each rider sported the vest with the wolf gang's insignia and a mirrored helmet hiding their identity. He wasn't scared at all by the display of power, but he knew he was on shaky ground with the spell over their land dampening his abilities. JT pulled off his helmet and stared at Israel, the power of his alpha wolf on full display. JT's eyes flashed between gold and the dark brown of his natural color, and his canines were peeking from between his lips. Energy crackled around the wolf, potent and dominant. Israel had to admit that he was impressed.

"We gon' have a problem, Israel?" He asked in a deep, growly voice full of his animal.

"I don't see why we need to have an issue. This is between my wife and me."

"You're on my grandmother's land, through shields that have held out stronger people," Ness said, descending the stairs. Her magic probed at his, and Israel allowed it. The sooner she realized he meant them no harm, the closer he was to seeing his wife.

"Audrey is mine, and nothing will keep me from her." He told them all.

Vanessa titled her head, a thoughtful expression covering her face. "I don't give a shit about your possessiveness. You on this land means something entirely different and if you're not ready for that, leave her the fuck alone."

Israel bristled, his magic tingling, responding to her tone.

"Inside, Fouche. You too, Ness," JT ordered the women.

Ness nodded and gave Israel a final sneering look before turning to do as asked. Israel's eyes followed because, yes, they were beautiful, but it was the power coming off of both women that had his attention. Their magic was off the charts.

JT whistled, pulling him from his thoughts. "Eyes back in your head."

"Their power is...something," He murmured, turning his attention to JT.

The wolf nodded. "Listen, Black. You stirring up all kinds of shit. What's the plan?"

"I want Audrey."

"That's it, huh?" JT chuckled and shook his head. "I take it you think throwing around your power is the way to go about it? You clearly ain't learn nothing about your mate in the time y'all been married. Otherwise, you'd know that lil' mama don't care about all that shit."

Israel gritted his teeth; that this man knew more about his wife than him didn't sit well with him.

"Let me hip you to some game right quick. Audrey ain't got no problem going lick for lick, understand? She returns energy times ten. You want war with her; you'll get it. All that magic shit aside, the fact that you're on her grandmother's land, still standing, means that she been being nice to your ass."

He studied the wolf, nodding for him to continue.

"She could've run you out of town at any moment. Yeah, you got power, but you ain't never dealt with a Fouche on their own territory. Going tit for tat is never going to work because when she gets fed up, you'll be ass out. Without your wife, and possibly your life. If you want soft with Lil mama, then you need to give her soft." JT put his helmet on, and revved the engine.

Israel held up his hand, and JT let off the gas and lifted the mirrored visor. "I've been tracked here to Springbrook."

The wolf nodded, understanding his meaning. "We got her."

JT nodded his head towards Israel's car, and Israel understood that he was being dismissed. Instead of taking offense, Israel thought over his words. Could dealing with Audrey be as simple as that? He was willing to try anything at this point. He looked into the side mirror, spotting the wolves escorting him from the Fouche property. Clearly, the way he'd been handling it wasn't working. Perhaps a different strategy was in order.

Chapter Seventeen

Audrey's mind was spinning as she came downstairs the next morning. Despite all the turmoil from the day before, she'd slept well. Her dreams were at the forefront of her mind all morning. There were so many questions she had about her grandmother's visit. She was relieved to see Nicole in the kitchen as soon as she rounded the corner. The perfect person to ask.

"You working?"

"Yeah, had some emergency stuff come up."

Audrey grabbed a glass to get water. For a minute or two, the only sound in the kitchen was Nic's typing. She was trying to figure out how to approach the subject of their grandmother. It wasn't like Nicole was hard to talk to. Audrey just didn't know where to start.

Nic chuckled. "You're staring a hole in the side of my head."

Audrey sighed. "I saw Grandmother last night."

Nic stopped typing and gave Audrey her full attention. "Last night?"

She sat across from Nic and nodded. "I felt her yesterday when I was at Iz's hotel."

"You felt her presence?"

"Mmhmm."

"What happened?"

"Israel told me he married me so he could have unfettered access to my power."

Nic sucked her teeth. "I should've slapped him harder."

Audrey gasped. Wait a damn minute. "When did you slap him?"

"Later. Finish your story about Grandmother."

She was still stuck on Nic slapping Israel. "Umm, right. I left him for good when the summons from Grandmother's lawyers came because when I met his grandmother, she had told me that Israel only married me to take my power. I guess now that I think about it, I already knew that he hadn't married me for the right reasons."

"Part of the family baggage you were talking about?" Nic asked. She nodded, and Nic hummed. "Why would his grandmother tell you that?"

Audrey frowned because it was a valid question. More than likely, the woman was stirring up trouble. She hadn't thought about it at the time. What kind of relationship did he have with his grandmother that she would go out of her way to sabotage his relationship?

"Think about it later, so, you ran...again? How many times had you run away from him?"

"For the four years that we've been married, I ran every time I started to feel something for him. I would stay a few months, start falling in love and run," she whispered, ashamed. She was no better than Israel when it came to making their marriage work.

Nic gave her a sympathetic look. "This curse is hell, Audrey. I'm sure you only wanted to protect him. Which I assumed made his betrayal that much worse."

She nodded, swallowing the lump in her throat. That she'd put herself through so much anguish to protect him and to find out that he didn't have any feelings for her...it hurt.

"And what did Israel say?"

"He said he never intended to carry out his grandmother's plan. But, he did plan to use me to build up his own power. He wants to expand his territory, and having access to my power will give him that."

"Interesting," Nic said.

"I got so mad and hurt that I left. I was sitting in the car, and I felt Grandmother. It gave me the strength to go back in and ask him to help us. Which he agreed to do."

"Well, it's in his best interest. You have feelings for him. That's all it takes for the curse to activate," Nic shrugged.

Audrey groaned and lowered her head to the table. So even that was selfish.

"So your dream about Grandmother," Nic prodded, turning the subject back to her original point.

"She told me I had to prep the family for the 'backlash that was coming.' What do you think that means?"

"You're like a savant with spells, Audrey. Seeing what you did with TiTi Shelby was amazing to witness. I think you should start working on the wards around this place. Israel got in easily enough last night."

Audrey's cheeks heated. "He came over last night?"

Nic nodded. "Came to 'get what was his', let him tell it."

Oh God. Her stomach dipped despite her anger at him, and her heart fluttered. "Wait...he got past the wards?"

"Him and his silent lion," Nic commented, studying her face. "Ooh, what did you do?"

"My cat," Audrey whispered. "She bonded with him a little bit, just a teeny bit, really. I didn't know it would allow him to get past the wards."

"So he is yours." Nicole hummed.

Audrey eyed her, and another thing grandmother said stood out. She sat up straight. "Grandmother said she gave you something to do."

Nic smiled. "Yeah, that slap was not why I went to his hotel. Grandmother picked JT for me...or not me in particular. She knew that he would be one of ours; she couldn't tell which one before she died. She set protections in place for him. She was murdered before she could do the same for you and Ness. She told me it was my responsibility."

"You gave Israel a jar?" Audrey felt some type of way about that, even though she was still mad at him.

"No, that's your job. Just give him the one you've already made. I made and carved a candle for him. It would be better if he got tattoos like JT, but the candle will work as long as he completes the ritual."

"Thank you, Nic."

"Of course. Are you going to talk to Aunt Kit?"

Audrey blew out a frustrated breath. "Am I the only one freaked out by what she did?"

"It threw me for a loop, I will admit." Nic conceded. "But she paid for it."

Audrey pressed her hands into her chest. "I paid for it, too."

"Yes, what you experienced can't be discounted. You shouldered a lot."

Audrey dropped her head. "This place was supposed to be a refuge. Why is all this emotional stuff being churned up?"

"Whew, now, you said a word," Nic told her and returned to her work. "We'll get through it."

Israel tapped his fingers along the top of the steering wheel and stared at the barrier over the Fouche land. He'd already proved he could get through it, but curiosity wouldn't let him leave it alone. He probed at the ward, once again impressed by the amount of magic and skill that had gone into it. The complex spell woven into it glowed in different hues, intertwined tightly. Proof that more than one person had worked on it. The more vivid colors had to be older, baked into the spell for longer. He would love to know what went into it.

It was rooted in the land that much he was sure about. The power of it rubbed against his personal boundaries. Little flickers of light popped off as the spell to suppress his magic activated. He waved his hand in awe, feeling the weight of it. He shook his head and pulled his magic back, resigning himself to the fact that he wouldn't be as strong on Fouche land.

As he pulled his magic back, his vision returned to normal. He could no longer see the shimmering wall over their property with his naked eye. Instead, he saw the dirt road leading to Patsy Fouche's home. He was stalling. Flat out. He needed to find the words to get Audrey to give him another chance. He'd fucked it up yesterday, but surely he was intelligent enough to convince his wife.

He almost wished he had Eli with him if only to talk shit and push him the last remaining feet. But, he'd forced his best friend to stay at the hotel, enduring his lecture and demands that Israel proceed with caution. As if he wouldn't.

Enough stalling.

He sighed and pushed down on the gas. Taking a deep breath, he drove the short distance to Audrey's grandmother's house. As he got out of the car, he could feel the power of the land. At one time, he would've killed to get access to that power. But at the end of the day, he'd rather have the woman.

He walked to the front door, skimming power as he ascended the steps. He couldn't help it. The magic was hypnotizing. He watched the power dance across his fingertips as he waited on someone to answer the door. This close to his wife, he could feel her presence on the other side. A moment later, the click of the locks disengaging sounded. He sucked in a sharp breath as Audrey answered the door.

She was wearing a tank top and short shorts. He'd seen her like that plenty of times before. The memory of it was so vivid that he could almost feel her soft skin on his palm as though he'd caressed her. She frowned down at his hands. Israel swallowed his growl, having been caught.

"What are you doing here?"

He extinguished the power still sparking on his skin and slid his hands into the pocket of his jeans. "I want to talk to you. No games."

She stared at him for a tense moment before stepping back and waving him inside. He nodded to Nicole, who narrowed her eyes at him in warning. Audrey took him past a workshop that was buzzing with power. They ended up sitting in a pair of wicker patio chairs in the backyard.

Audrey wrapped a blanket around herself and sat silently next to him, waiting on him to speak. His eyes raked over the backyard, impressed with the greenhouse and small garden. Power saturated every corner of their property. The yard stretched back a few feet before stopping at a dense forest. It was a peaceful magic that seeped into him as he settled in the chair.

"I want to first apologize for the way I pursued you. It started off selfish, yes, but as I got to know you, it changed."

"When? When did it change?"

He grimaced because she would ask him that. They stared each other down.

"Here."

"So when you came to Georgia, you had every intention of using me for power?"

He was speechless. What did he say that wouldn't hurt her more than he already had?

"I think it was a mix of both. When you left this last time, a part of me was angry, and I wanted you back. I wanted access to your power, yes, but more than that, I wanted you."

She stared at him, her eyes roaming his face. He felt the light touch of her magic as she probed his thoughts. He let her have it. His feelings, his longing, all of it. He gave it to her freely. JT told him to give her soft, and he would do that if it would bring her back to him.

She cleared her throat and crossed her arms over her chest. "And now? What do you want?"

"I want another chance at our relationship." He didn't embellish. He didn't think charm would get him out of this situation.

"The curse is still hanging over our family. It's dangerous for us even to consider getting back together."

It wasn't a no.

He let out a relieved breath and settled more comfortably in the chair. "I can help with that."

"Did you light the candle Nic gave you?"

He smiled and rubbed his cheek, nodding. "Your cousin don't play about you."

Audrey snorted. "I don't know if I'm ready for the rollercoaster of you, Lucky."

"Tell me why you ran all those times before?" They'd both been on a rollercoaster their entire marriage. She was not without fault in that. "The real reason, Audrey."

From the wince on her face, she caught the implication of his question.

"Let me first ask you something. Did you agree to help me because you don't want the curse to affect you?"

He frowned. "What do you mean?"

"The curse affects the people we love," she told him.

His heart stuttered, and everything within him stilled. "You love me?"

Chapter Eighteen

"You love me?" He whispered it again.

Such a devastated, relieved look covered his face that Audrey paused. He thought she didn't care for him? That was totally on her then because she'd been hiding from it herself. She thought about her grandmother's words. Had she missed something in his words to her?

"Lucky," she sighed. "This curse has not missed a single woman in our family."

He sat up, his dark eyes spearing her. "After the bear attack. You left because you thought it was the curse?"

She nodded.

"Kitty cat, I get into danger all on my own. That has nothing to do with you. Plus, I handled it like I do everything else." The sinister smile that covered his face reminded her of how dangerous her husband was.

She shuddered because she remembered hearing what had happened to those bears.

He lifted his head and looked to the sky. "The vampire attack? You left right after then, too," he murmured to himself. He turned to her, "after the turf war between the other practitioner and me. You left to 'check on your mother.' You...you were leaving to protect me?"

She turned her head. "I know your power, Israel, but it seemed like every time I came back, there was someone or something else gunning for you. Little accidents, spell mistakes, I didn't want you hurt."

He smiled and approached her, dropping to his knees in front of her chair. He grabbed the back of her neck. "I'm a little embarrassed to admit this, but you make me nervous, Audrey. I can't think straight when you're close to me. Sometimes when I smell your scent, my concentration is shot. It doesn't help that you would sit on my work bench in just my shirt, swinging your sexy ass legs. Do you imagine there wouldn't be mistakes with my spell work?"

Her heart tripped. "Lucky," she whispered.

He nuzzled into the side of her neck. "And that," he said, kissing her skin. "Your voice, the way you say my name. Ain't no work getting done when you're around, love."

He pulled her chin down and kissed her, stealing her air. The man was potent. Her body melted, pliant in his arms. He pulled back.

"It took me a while to realize my feelings for you. I was in denial for a long time. I kept making up excuses for why I had to have you in my life, but bottom line is that I miss you." He pecked her lips softly. "I need you."

She slid her hand over his hair, desire and love making her hands shake. Their lack of communication had caused the rift in their relationship, yes, but the fact of the matter was that the curse was still active and could still affect their lives.

"I don't want anything to happen to you, Lucky." She laid her cheek against his.

"I got that nickname for a reason, love." He laughed, lifting her from the chair and sitting. He pulled her down into his lap. "I'm not worried about a curse."

She sighed and relaxed in his arms. "If we can break it, it would mean so much for this family. It's caused so much strife."

He dropped soft kisses along her shoulders. "I'll do whatever I can to help."

She turned to face him. "And us?"

"You have to be in this with me. I've chased you all over this god-forsaken country, but if you're not willing to meet me halfway, then this is already dead. The in and out stops. I require loyalty from anyone who works for me, I won't allow less for the woman who holds my heart, and I won't give you any less than I demand."

Their eyes met, the heat between them burning. But, she saw his determination, his earnestness. She had to have faith in her ability. Both her grandmother and her cousins had faith in her magic; surely, she could break the curse and keep her husband. Israel didn't rush her, instead waiting her out. He didn't even probe her mind, allowing her to come to a decision on her own. She could see what his patience was costing him.

"You need me to beg? That ain't my way at all, but for you, kitty cat, I might be tempted," he whispered softly against her neck.

Chills ran down her spine at the contact. She didn't need him to beg, he'd let her into his mind, and she could discern his sincerity. That he'd come to her was a big step on his part. From his reputation and the things she'd observed, her husband didn't bow to anyone. He certainly never chased or begged for anything when his brute magic had been enough to bring those in his territory to heel. It had to count for something that he put it all aside to pursue her. She nodded.

She would stick this out with him.

"Thank fuck," he whispered, devouring her mouth.

He nibbled his way down her neck to the bodice of her shirt. He pinched her nipple, smiling as she shuddered in his arms. He pushed her shirt down, exposing her breast to his greedy gaze.

"Not out here," she whispered, even as she arched her back to give him better access.

She could never resist Israel. Her body was his and had been from the very first moment he touched her.

Israel chuckled and moved her shirt back, standing with her in his arms. Audrey wrapped her legs around his waist, holding on for dear life. She held her breath as they entered the house and directed him upstairs to her room. The last thing she wanted was her cousins catching her. Not that it would stop her, but it would be slightly embarrassing.

Audrey closed her room door behind them with her foot, and Israel wasted no time. He spun her until her back was against the wall next to the door. She felt his magic gathering, chuckling when her clothes disappeared from her body.

"Impatient, are we?"

He grunted in answer, sucking her nipple into his mouth. She moaned, throwing her head back. His clothes disappeared next, and she squirmed as she felt the warm steel of his dick against her center.

"Tell me again," he demanded, lifting his head to meet her eyes.

She knew what he wanted. She cupped both cheeks, giving him her undivided attention. "I love you."

He growled, surging forward, entering her. Audrey sighed in relief, even though he had to work himself into her wet center. She'd missed him just as much as he had her. His every stroke hit nerve endings that sent her spiraling in pleasure. She braced her feet on his hips, using the leverage to ride him. She wanted all of him, every inch he had to offer.

"Just like that, sweets," he encouraged, gripping her hips tightly.

The pain added another layer to the sex. She kissed him, sucking on his tongue as he fucked her with deep, long strokes. She closed her eyes, savoring his presence and rocking her hips into his. She released her magic, removing the barriers over her mind that she had put up. He rushed to fill the space, taking over both her mind and body. Heat filled her as his magic played with hers, blending and swirling until she couldn't tell where she left off, and he began.

"Israel," she moaned, arching her back. "I'm almost there."

"Just a little longer, kitten. You're doing so well. You feel incredible," he whispered in her ear.

She didn't know if she had a little longer left. Between his magic encompassing her and the way his groin slid against her clit, she was near the edge. Israel pulled out, and she growled. He laughed, turning her around until they met the bed. He laid her gently, turning her on her side. He lifted her leg and slid back inside.

She moaned loudly.

"You like that, don't you? Of course, you do," he murmured, nipping at her ear, relaxing his pace.

It didn't matter, though. Her body was so primed that even his breath brushing against her neck spun her higher. She reached back and gripped the back of his head, bringing him to her for a kiss. Israel's kiss was gentle, loving. With them so tightly bound, his every emotion was open to her. She gasped as realization crashed over her.

"You love me," she whispered.

"With everything in me," he confirmed, driving his hips into hers.

He gripped the front of her throat and squeezed. Stars burst behind her closed lids as he hit her g spot. The orgasm that crashed over her couldn't have been avoided even if she wanted to. Pleasure filled her to overflow. The strangled cry that left her throat could hardly be called a scream. Israel chuckled, kissing her neck.

"Such a good girl," he panted as he pounded into her. "My good girl."

His body tensed, and she felt a warm tide as he came. He kissed her shoulder, holding her tightly against him.

"Say it again," he whispered.

She snorted. "You say it. I had to go in your head to find out."

"I love you." He used his finger to nudge her chin back to him.

The kiss he gave her left no room for doubt of his feelings. She sighed as he pulled back. Israel left the bed, and she heard the water in her en suite a moment later. She relaxed but frowned as she took stock of her body. She could still feel his magic moving around within her body. Israel turned her onto her back and parted her legs. He was gentle as he cleaned off her sex. He leaned down and kissed her inner thigh as he finished, tossing the washcloth over his shoulder.

"Israel?"

"Yes, my love?" His warm breath caressed her skin.

She pushed against his head. "Wait."

He growled but sat up, quirking one eyebrow up in question.

"Do you feel my magic?" She searched his face as he frowned.

His frown didn't last long. His face cleared before a full-blown smile covered his face. "We're bonded."

She nodded, fear taking over momentarily. There was no more running from the curse.

He cupped her cheek, coming up to lay beside her. He pulled her into his chest. "We're going to break the curse, kitty cat. Stop over-thinking before your anxiety spirals."

It was easier said than done. Now, both her and Nicole's relation-ships depended on her, and she was scared shitless.

Chapter Nineteen

Israel scrubbed a hand over the top of his hair as he descended the stairs the following day. He'd showered and now wore a t-shirt and basketball shorts, courtesy of his wife having stolen his clothes before she left. He smiled because they now smelled like her. He wondered how often she'd worn them. Did she take them to think of him when they were apart? He'd have to ask her.

His body was exhausted, but in that way that only great sex made it. Audrey had been gone by the time he woke, but he felt her on the property, so he wasn't worried. That was new. They'd reached a new level of their relationship last night because he had to use his magic to search her out before. Now, she was a warm weight in his mind, and if needed, he could pinpoint her exact location.

He smiled triumphantly.

They were bonded, and it felt amazing. He followed the smell of coffee into the kitchen and spotted a woman who looked exactly like Audrey, except older. They had the same pert nose, full lips, and dark, heavily lashed eyes. The woman's face was scrubbed free of makeup and with gentle crinkles around her eyes which meant she spent a lot of time squinting her eyes....

Kind of like she was doing now as she watched him.

"You must be Audrey's mother." He spoke first, sitting across from her at the small table tucked into the breakfast nook.

The woman studied him over her cup of coffee. "Are you another guard sent by this mysterious husband?"

His smile was full of charm because he wanted this first meeting with her mother to go well. "I am the mysterious husband."

Her eyes widened in surprise, but she recovered quickly. "Well, have you got a name?"

"I'm Israel Black," he held out his hand.

"Deleon," Audrey corrected as she came around the corner.

"I don't go by that name," he said, pulling his wife into his lap.

He closed his eyes, soaking in the feel of her. Her magic was bubbling around her as though she'd just finished a spell. It was a bright, happy magic. He wondered what she had been doing since she'd left bed this morning.

"All the same," she said. "My mother should know exactly who you are." She stood. "Mama, my husband, Israel Deleon, Lucky, my mama, Kit Marks. Now, do you want breakfast?"

"Please," he said, studying his wife.

What he really wanted was to take her back to bed. But her mother watched their interaction, her eyes taking in every nuance.

"I can tell by your aura that you use questionable magic." Kit finally said.

"Mama," Audrey warned.

Kit pinched her lips tight. "What? I can't ask the man questions?"

Audrey sighed and continued with her preparations. He had a personal chef at home, so it was the first time she had cooked for him. He found himself touched by the mundane gesture.

Kit knocked on the table, dragging his attention back to her. "Questionable magic," she reminded him.

Israel shrugged. "I like power."

"Like it or need it?" She squinted her eyes and studied him.

That was a little too close to the truth. He could feel her magic probing him. It wasn't as strong as his wife's. It almost felt disjointed. He could tell there was some type of trauma there. It intrigued him. He allowed her to probe if only to get a better taste of her magic. While she got a feel for him, he examined the source of chaos within her. It had the taste of magic gone wrong. There were jagged light points throughout her aura.

She pulled back and sucked her teeth. "Did you see what you wanted?"

He smiled, his usual charming smile.

She waved her hand. "That won't work on me, baby. I'm not sleeping with you."

Audrey cursed and dropped the frozen sausage onto the counter. Before she could say something, Ness came around the corner. He'd researched her family after Nicole had come to see him. He wanted information on all of her cousins to know what he was dealing with. Vanessa Fouche had been caught up in legal troubles not long ago. He was curious to know how much her cousins knew about it. He, himself, had been surprised by what he'd learned. He would keep his mouth shut for now because it wasn't his business.

Ness stared at him and then her aunt before shaking her head and turning to Audrey. "Lord, Audrey, you can't cook an entire breakfast in the air fryer."

Kit raised her hands. "Don't look at me. We don't cook on this side. I can't judge my baby on how she learned to fend for herself."

He felt Audrey's embarrassment and a grain of something darker. He wondered the story behind that. In the years they were married, she hadn't talked about her family except to say when she was visiting them. Tension coated the kitchen, and Israel wondered where it stemmed. It wasn't as though Audrey shared a lot with him. They needed to rectify that this go around. Audrey gave him a look he couldn't decipher. Maybe things were being shared she wasn't ready for him to hear.

Nicole came in next from the front door. "Morning, what's going on?" She looked at Israel. "Well, that didn't take long."

"So you not even going to pretend tact," Ness said dryly.

"Chill, it's too early, and me and Mr. Black have an understanding," Nicole said with a smirk.

He raised a brow.

"You lit that candle?"

"I did," he answered. He'd brought the candle with him to ask Audrey about last night. She'd just reiterated to him that he needed to light it since they were going to give their marriage a try. Israel mentally reached out to his wife, *"is it always like this?"*

"Every morning," she told him.

He studied her. *"You feel happy here. Is that what you were missing? Family?"*

The look she gave him clenched his heart. He wanted to take her home immediately, especially with Annabelle in the state and setting up at the family estate. It was his grandmother's power center. She was at her most dangerous there. She usually traveled while Arianne was in school, stopping into Savannah monthly to renew her power. That she had been home this long was troubling.

But, he could feel the bubbles of happiness around his wife. He needed to think about that. Would she be happy with only visits to her cousins?

Audrey felt Ness's gaze. Her cousin's curious thoughts broadcast easily. She didn't answer the question swirling in Ness' mind. Instead, turning back to her sausage in the air fryer.

"You want pancakes, cousin-in-law?" Nic asked.

Audrey groaned because not everyone understood Nicole's dry humor.

"So long as you don't poison them." He answered in the same sarcastic tone.

Nic snickered.

"Hell nah, I'm not dealing with two of you," Ness complained.

Israel tilted his head in question.

"You have the same weird sense of humor as Nic," Audrey answered his unspoken question.

He scoffed in her head and withdrew.

"Wait, y'all, can talk telepathically?" Kit asked, surprised.

"Stay out of my head, mama," Audrey fussed.

Kit sighed. "So you plan on being mad at me forever."

"Jesus Christ, Katherine, it's been less than two days," Lauren said as she came in a step in front of the other aunts.

"Stay out of it, Lauren," Dawn warned.

That warning slid off Lauren's shoulders. "Let the damn girl be. She has a right to her feelings."

"You worry about your daughter, and I'll worry about mine." Kit snapped.

"A little later than scheduled, but right on time," Nicole muttered, taking eggs out of the fridge. "You making sausages?"

"Yep," Audrey said. "You want bacon too?"

"Please," Ness answered as she started cutting up fruit.

The three of them made food while their mamas finished their usual bickering. She cut a look at Israel. He looked on in amusement, relaxed in the chair. The arguing clearly did not bother him. She slid him a cup of coffee, and he gripped her chin, pulling her down for a kiss.

"You okay?"

"This don't bother me, kitten." He pecked her lips.

"Unh-Unh, what this is?" Dawn waved her hand between Audrey and Israel. The arguing had stopped, and the sisters' eyes were on them.

Audrey sighed and stood straight, ignoring the snickers from her cousins. "This is my husband, Israel." She made quick introductions.

"Wait until we eat before y'all start showing out," Ness pleaded.

Reluctantly her aunts agreed, but they eyed him, three different kinds of magic probing at his aura. Audrey sighed and went back to cooking. It was going to be a long morning.

Chapter Twenty

Audrey needed a break.

Despite Ness' warning, her aunts had questioned Israel throughout the entirety of breakfast. Her husband was clever, though, because his answers revealed nothing about him that she hadn't already known. He was from Savannah. His aunt still lived there with his little sister. He'd made no mention of his grandmother, which she found odd. He never did now that she thought about it. It was why the woman's visit had been so startling. Adding in the information, she'd so gleefully imparted to Audrey, it was starting to make sense.

Israel told her family that he ran a mergers and acquisitions firm and left out his after-hours job as a warlock who controlled most of Miami's illegal magic. She didn't blame him, though. Her mother would've probably thrown a fit if she knew. Israel had handled it all with calm amusement. He touched her mind, sliding a gentle hand across her arm as she grabbed the dishes from the table. He'd been doing that all morning.

Touching her.

It was such a change from how he treated her before; it was

throwing her off. He was more affectionate...softer. She liked it, but it made her a little wary. When would the other Israel come back out? The one who demanded more than he asked? His phone rang, and he stood.

"I need to take this, love." He told her before stepping out.

All eyes turned to her. She sighed and started cleaning the table. All that curiosity they'd had for Israel was now aimed at her.

"How in the hell did you end up marrying this man?" Aunt Dawn asked.

A lump clogged her throat as she recalled the night she'd met Israel. She'd been drinking at a bar on the anniversary of her father's death. She'd been several shots in when Israel had walked up to her. His swagger had caught her attention before she'd made her way up to his handsome face. Something about him had called to her. Somehow she didn't think her family would want to know that marrying Israel had been a drunken impulse.

"He swept me off my feet," she half-lied.

That sentiment seemed so tame for the insatiable need that Israel ignited within her. At her first glance of him, her whole being had settled. How could she describe seeing him and just knowing instinctually that he was her person? It wasn't until her sober brain had caught up to the implications of what her feelings meant that she'd gotten scared. She spent the first years of their marriage so frightened of her feelings for him.

"Does he know his family is the one who cursed us?" Aunt Lauren's question brought her out of her musings.

She nodded. "He's going to help us break it."

Her mother looked suspicious. Not that Audrey blamed her.

"How are we going to do this?" Nicole asked.

"I have a few ideas," Israel said, rejoining them in the kitchen. He leaned his shoulder against the wall. "I can't get access to the actual spell, but my great grandfather hid a counter spell and the original token they used to cast the spell."

"What kind of token?" Aunt Shelby frowned.

Israel shrugged. "It can be anything of Rose's, from a piece of her clothing to a lock of her hair. I won't know until I find it."

"How do you know about this token?" Kit asked.

"The men in my family kept a journal. They spent their lives trying to control their wives, sisters, and mothers. The women in our family were single-minded in their pursuit of magic. According to Jacob, the token was kept as an insurance policy." Israel told them.

"Insurance for what?" Audrey asked.

He stared at her, his eyes boring into her. His hunger for her, his love, all of it broadcasted across their new bond. It was overwhelming for a moment. The feelings she had for him before paled in comparison to whatever this was.

Ness cleared her throat, and it broke into their moment.

Israel smiled. "When Henry died, Jacob took it so that his mother would know that if they went too far, he could always reverse the spell over the Fouche's."

The kitchen was silent as they all absorbed his words.

"And after all this time? Does it still serve as insurance?" Nic asked.

Guilt filled him, and he looked away. "The women in your family hold an incredible amount of innate power. My family wanted it for themselves. When your Rose wouldn't marry Henry, they took it. Or rather, they changed it. Shifted it into the power of your cat so that the root workers in our family could access it for themselves. Cats are our animals to call."

Aunt Dawn cursed. "Is that why we can't control the cats?"

"You weren't meant to be able to control it. It binds your magic within it." He admitted.

"Fuck," Ness whispered. "Tell me your family's side of this?"

Israel moved to the kitchen table and sat. "According to Jacob, my great-grandfather, Henry, and Rose, were working on establishing this town. It was supposed to be a haven for all paranormals. Both our families founded it and put magic into protecting it from outsiders.

The two of them were the strongest magic users at the time. They worked together on the ward that was supposed to cover the town."

"And Henry fell in love with Rose," Aunt Shelby muttered.

Israel nodded. "According to the women in our family, Rose broke Henry's heart. Sent him spiraling down a dark path of dark magic."

Nic squinted her eyes. "You don't believe that?"

Israel scoffed. "I know the women in my family. More than likely, they were the ones who urged Henry down that path." He sighed. "Either way, when Rose turned him down, my family left to establish their own town."

"Except, they didn't have the magic the Fouche's had?" Aunt Lauren said.

"Not even close. Like I said, your magic is innate and strong after generations of cultivating it. My family deals in arcane magic. Knowing the inner workings of Rose's magic, Henry decided that stealing the Fouche's magic would both get back at Rose and solve their problems."

"Oh, fuck your family, Israel," Ness muttered.

Audrey held up her hand. "Hold on, so what about the love portion of the curse?"

"You mentioned that yesterday. I don't understand," Israel answered.

"Any person who falls in love with the women in our family dies, or at least they do if they don't leave first. There hasn't been a woman since my grandmother that has been able to keep a relationship without dire consequences." Aunt Shelby told him. "Not to mention the obsession with them. We've had some domestic issues behind it."

It was his turn to frown. "That's not what I read about the curse."

"So, Henry's sisters added it to the spell without his knowledge?" Nic asked.

"Henry didn't survive the spell. His sisters took over. Jacob wrote that Henry's sisters had changed the curse, but he didn't know the particulars. He couldn't get a straight answer out of anyone, but he dropped it since he said it wouldn't affect the efficacy of the counter-spell. But, even I wouldn't have guessed they'd do something that… heinous."

Aunt Shelby raised her hand. "Wait. Henry died during a spell. According to my grandmother, his sisters came here and accused Rose of being the reason he killed himself."

"That's not what Jacob said. My grandmother doesn't talk about it, so I can only go by his journal."

They all shared a look.

Israel felt the tension gathering in the room. The women were pissed, and he wasn't sure it was a good idea for him to stick around while they were in that head space.

He reached out to his wife. "*Maybe we can take a walk and give your aunts time to process?*"

She nodded and walked towards the front door. "Israel and I are going out for a walk." She announced to the room.

He followed her from the room, breathing easy once they were outside. "I'm not sure if it will be safe for me to go back in there," he half-joked.

Audrey sighed. "It's a lot to take in."

He reached down and grabbed her hand. Audrey threaded her fingers with his, and they walked into the woods surrounding the property. There was a worn path, so he assumed it was one her family took often. The cool air brushed against his skin, and he murmured a quick spell, encapsulating them in a circle of warmth. She looked up at him and smiled.

"You deflected many of my mother's questions this morning," she told him.

He chuckled. "A habit. However, I'm an open book to you. What do you want to know?"

She touched his mind lightly, her magic a warm breeze. "When we were at the hotel, you mentioned that your job in the family was to get magic for them. What does that mean?"

He instantly regretted his vow to be truthful with her.

"Truth, Lucky. If we're going to do this, we need to have all our cards on the table," she said softly.

He turned to her and cupped her cheek. "You won't like my answer."

She grabbed his hand. "I dreamed of my grandmother. She told me that together, the two of us could be a force."

Shocked, he had nothing to say to that. That her powerful grandmother was rooting for them even from the other side intimidated him, he felt pressured to get it right. Her thumb caressed his bottom lip.

"Talk to me, Lucky."

He grabbed her hand and nuzzled into her palm, dreading what he had to tell her. He sighed and dropped his hand. She intertwined their fingers. Her face was expectant, and Israel knew his time had run out.

"The ritual I told you about, the one we use to take power from others? It's a part of our deal with the goddess Kisasi. In exchange for boosting our power, a percentage of the power we take is funneled back to her."

"So it's not just me?" Her eyes were wide.

He shook his head. "Every month on the full moon, I have to complete the ritual."

She gasped and took a step back. "You've been...stealing powers from other practitioners?"

"I don't have a choice," he told her.

Her eyes roamed his face, her mind spinning. He could almost see the thoughts tumbling over each other. What he didn't see was fear. That gave him some hope.

"What happens if you don't?"

"Kisasi will get her cut of the power regardless. Whether she has to take it from us directly or indirectly from the ceremony."

She shuddered. "Why do you have to be the one to do it?"

Israel ran a hand over his hair. "If not me, it would've been my little sister."

Chapter Twenty-One

er heart hurt for him. She was in the back of his mind, his every emotion open to her. She could feel what he was trying to hide behind the stoic look on his face. He still feared for his sister. Audrey stepped closer to him.

"Explain."

Israel pulled her into his arms and nuzzled his face against her neck. He breathed her in, tension tightening his body. He felt like a steel band in her arms; he was so stiff.

"Arianne was eight when it was time for my family to renew the covenant. I couldn't allow my little sister to go through it. She's the purest thing in my life, or at least she was before you," he whispered, settling his forehead against hers.

"Iz." She gave him a soft kiss.

She stepped back and grabbed his hand, pulling him forward. They walked in silence for a little while. Her mind was spinning with all the questions she wanted to ask him.

"What happens to your sister if you stop?"

He growled under his breath. "My grandmother holds her safety over my head every chance she gets."

"In what way?" She stopped and swung around to face him.

"My mother only had Arianne after pressure from my grand-mother. There's a certain point where the family vas ages out, and she didn't think the men in our family were strong enough to renew the covenant. So, she forced my mother to have another child, hoping it would be a girl. My mother didn't have Arianne in time, though." He started walking again.

"Mama died giving birth to my sister. It threw all of Annabelle's carefully laid plans out of whack. My mother was supposed to take over for Annabelle until Arianne came of age. My aunt Sabine doesn't have the power needed to make the covenant. It took me years to realize that was on purpose. It was her only rebellion against my grandmother."

She noted the lack of affection when he talked about his grand-mother. He always called her by her first name. In contrast, he was a little more reverent when he spoke of his mother. Was he still grieving for her? She sped her steps to keep up with his long stride. He was lost in his story and not paying attention to how fast he was walking.

"From the first moment I laid eyes on my sister, I fell in love. I couldn't let the foulness of my grandmother rub off on her. Between me and my aunt Sabine, we managed to shelter her from as much as possible. But, without mama, the power dipped faster than Annabelle anticipated. It was time to renew the covenant, and she didn't have the power to do so. She was going to use Arianne, although her power wasn't nearly developed enough. I stepped in her place."

"Oh, Lucky," she murmured, rubbing a hand down his arm.

"If I don't make the monthly sacrifices, then Annabelle will just use Arianne to replace me." He told her.

Her heart stuttered, feeling his fear and helpless frustration. "You left. Is there a way we can get your sister away from there?"

He grabbed her and lifted her so quickly it startled her. She wrapped her legs around his waist and held tight to his shoulders. His tortured eyes stared into hers, and she felt his magic inundate her, his feelings swamping her.

"You said 'we.'" He swooped down and devoured her mouth. Lust, love, and gratitude poured from him.

Audrey wrapped her arms around his neck and angled her head to deepen their kiss. She rode the wave of his emotions, tangling her fingers in his hair. He moaned, his tongue sliding against hers.

"Need you."

"We're outside."

"Don't care." He bit down on her bottom lip before sucking it into his mouth.

She chuckled. "I care."

He groaned, nipping at her ear. "You think of us as 'we.' That's a good sign."

"I told you, I'm in this with you. If we break this curse, then there's nothing stopping us from being together."

"Even if I have to keep making the sacrifices?"

She studied his face. At the end of the day, she understood that her husband wasn't what some would call a good guy. He liked the power he held over the people under him, and she imagined that though he'd initially stepped up to protect his sister, some part of him probably enjoyed the rush of power.

"I'm going to find a way to stop that too. I won't let you continue to weigh down your soul with it," she swore.

His eyes lit. "You know how I feel about amassing power."

She sighed. "There's always another way. A less dangerous way."

"And if I like the danger?" He dropped kisses along her jaw.

She groaned this time. "I'm under no illusion that I can completely reform you."

He laughed and set her down on her feet. "For you, I would do a lot of things that are out of character for me. I mean, look at me in the backwoods of Georgia."

"Not too much on my family's home." She smacked his arm, hiding her smile.

"Until I can safely remove Arianne from Annabelle, the sacrifices have to continue."

She could feel his regret, the heavy weight of the duty on his shoulders. She would find a way to get him out of it. She refused to let Israel continue to carry the burden.

"Jesus, did you two walk to California?" Ness asked as soon as they stepped back into their house.

Audrey rolled her eyes at her cousin's dramatics. "We just needed a moment."

"Well, did you think of a plan while you were out?" Nic asked.

JT had arrived at the house and was sitting on the floor between Nicole's legs. He eyed Israel, giving her a smirk before turning back to the T.V.

"Israel said something about a token. I want to know about that," Ness said.

"Where did mom go?" Audrey asked, settling in the armchair across from Nicole.

Israel lifted her and then pulled her back down into his lap.

"In the kitchen," Kit said as she came back.

"The token," Ness said impatiently.

"Jacob has the location of it hidden. If I can find the location, then we can use the token to possibly reverse the curse. We could maybe reverse the curse without it, but having the original piece of whatever it is will almost guarantee it." Israel told them.

"How do we find the location?" Aunt Shelby asked.

"This is where it will get tricky. Jacob wrote down its location in the family almanac. He disguised in the mundane notations on the plantation's crop growth. I normally wouldn't have access to it, but the Savannah Museum of History is putting on an exhibit for Black

History Month. They've asked my family to be a part of it since we're one of the oldest Black families in the area." Israel said.

He was rubbing her back in slow circles, and she was squirming in his lap, fighting to keep her heated body under control. He smiled down at her knowing good and damn well what he was doing.

"Wait. We got one of those invitations," Aunt Shelby said, sitting straight up. "I was just talking to Lauren about it. Cellus thinks we should do it. They've also asked a few of the old families from here."

"If his family will be there, I don't know that it's safe for us to do that," Aunt Dawn cautioned.

"My aunt promised to ensure the almanac is in the exhibition. It'll be hard, but I should be able to get access to the book there."

"Won't your grandmother be watching you?" Audrey said, frowning.

"I'm still working on the details," he said reluctantly. "If I can steal the book outright, that would be best. But, even a peek at the passages will work."

"We could help," Aunt Lauren spoke up.

"With what, the power of your bougie-ness?" Nic asked.

"Get your mate before I hurt her feelings, Jeremiah," Aunt Lauren said, tossing her hair over her shoulders. "I know people, for your information, Nicole."

Nic snorted. "Now that I believe."

"Cut it out, you two," Kit murmured absently.

Audrey could sense her mother's mind going, knowing she had an idea. "What is it, mama?"

"Well, powers aside. Going on Deleon turf is risky. But, us showing up could be a suitable enough distraction."

Israel stiffened beneath her. "You're right. My grandmother would be pissed that you were invited in the first place."

"If we go together, we should be safe enough," Aunt Lauren said.

"If we're doing this, we'll need an airtight plan," JT said from his spot on the floor. "It's not that I don't mind tearing some shit up behind y'all, but going into another alpha's territory will tie my hands."

"Not to step on any toes, but Nicole and Vanessa can't come. I don't think it would be a good idea to let Annabelle know you two even exist. She went after Audrey immediately after spotting her. I'm almost afraid of what she'd do to get her hands on either of you," he reluctantly said.

Audrey sat up straight. "I'm going."

He sighed. *"Kitten."*

She sliced her hand in the air. *"I'm not even arguing with you about it. I'm going."* She turned back to her family. "But, I agree with you about Nic and Ness," She said aloud.

"Well, that's bullshit," Ness grumbled.

They all shared a look. It took a few more minutes of arguing, but Nic and Ness finally agreed to allow just the aunts to go. It took another hour to hash out their plans. They were going to steal from a museum...under the watchful eye of a powerful witch. What was the worst thing that could happen?

Chapter Twenty-Two

Israel followed Audrey upstairs to her room, his eyes never leaving the sway of her hips. With every hour they spent together, he got a different perspective on her. Sitting in the same room with her and her cousins showed a different side to Audrey than he'd witnessed when they lived together. She was more relaxed, less...inhibited around them than she had been at home.

Could it be as simple as Audrey being comfortable? Could that change the course of their marriage?

And then, with her aunts and mother, was yet another side of her. She was a little more cautious with her words, and some underlying tension between her and Kit dimmed the bright spark that was usually in her eyes. He wanted to know what that was about but was unsure how to bring it up.

She pulled him into her bedroom and into her arms. Resting her head on his chest, she took a deep breath, her body going pliant in his arms.

"Dealing with your mother takes it out of you, huh?" He smiled and kissed the top of her head.

She groaned. "We'll get through it." She pulled back and brought his head down to her lips.

"Will you come back to the hotel with me?" he whispered against her lips.

"Can we stay here? I'll be more comfortable." She looked up at him.

Looking into those eyes of hers, he couldn't say no. He trailed a finger down her face before leaning over and giving her a soft kiss. "I'll need at least Eli here."

"There's plenty of space, at least for him. Not so much for the twins. But I don't think you need a full security team here anyway. I'll protect you." She grinned.

He snorted and kissed her again, unable to stop himself. She tiptoed, and he gripped the nape of her neck.

"My baby," he whispered, dropping soft kisses across her face.

She enthralled him until he could think of nothing else but her. There had been whole nights after she left him that he didn't sleep. And when he did, it was only to find her and walk through her dreams. The feelings that overwhelmed him when he was in her presence weren't healthy, but he cared less with every glide of her tongue over his. He walked forward, nudging her towards the bed, sucking her bottom lip into his mouth.

Her smile warmed him from the inside. Audrey dropped to her knees, and Israel held his breath as she slid down his shorts. Her hand wrapped around his erection, and she licked her lips. His eyelids dropped low as he watched her take him into her mouth. She held his gaze as her tongue darted out, teasing the head of his dick. She descended slowly, and he held his breath until he touched the back of her throat.

Fuck, she felt amazing.

"You're so perfect," he told her, caressing the side of her face as she swallowed him whole.

Her pouty lips mesmerized him. Watching his erection disappear into her mouth had his knees weak. He needed inside of her now. He pulled her up, smiling when she pouted in disappointment.

"I want in," he told her.

Audrey quickly chucked her clothes, getting into the middle of the bed. She beckoned to him, and Israel couldn't help but answer. He slid his body up hers, sighing in pleasure. She wrapped her arms around him and squeezed him tightly.

"I missed you," she whispered in his ear. "I'm not sure if I told you that or not."

He slid forward, her wet sex welcoming him. He reached for her mind, her magic answering his call immediately. He felt at peace as he fully seated his dick into her. She was his peace, his center, and there was nothing he would let come between them. His strokes were slow and decadent as he luxuriated in her. He was in no rush.

She moaned in his ear, her hands caressing his skin, her power filling every empty space her absence had left. Every moment of loneliness was worth the feeling of being in her arms again, wholly accepted for who he was.

"There's no part of you that isn't mine," she insisted, reading his thoughts.

She canted her hips into his, meeting his every push forward. Their lovemaking was slow, their whispers of love and devotion the only noise in their bubble of magic. If it took the rest of his life, he would show Audrey that she belonged to him, with him. They were one now, and he wouldn't have it any other way.

Audrey took a drowsy look around her dark room, unsure what had awakened her. It only took a moment for her to realize that Israel's thrashing had done it. He whimpered again, his body drenched in sweat as his muscles tensed. Her heart raced as she reached for him, worry for him waking her up fully. She touched his chest, and he gasped, sitting straight up. His eyes were foggy and unfocused. Sleep still had him in its clutches. She straddled him and cupped his cheeks.

"I'm here, love," she whispered, using her magic to wake him completely.

It took a moment before he focused his gaze on her. Audrey's heart stopped at the fear in his eyes before he masked it. He cleared his throat and ran a hand down his face.

"Shit, I'm sorry, kitten."

"No, don't apologize. Are you okay?" She asked him.

He nuzzled his head between her neck and shoulder, wrapping his arms around her. She hugged him back, using her magic to send soothing energy to him. It took a few minutes, but eventually, his body relaxed in her arms. She rubbed his back with one hand, massaging his neck with the other. He sighed and pulled back.

He kissed her softly. "Thank you, love."

"Nightmare?"

He nodded but didn't elaborate. In the years that she'd been married to him and the months when she'd actually stayed with him, he had nightmares a lot. Usually, she would let him get away with not answering, but she wanted better for their marriage now.

"Tell me, Lucky." She ran her hand through his beard, bringing his lips to her. "Talk to me, baby."

She kissed him softly, probing his mind to gauge his emotional state. She found him calm even though he was still a bit shaken.

"The same way I'm able to walk through your dreams, my grandmother can do the same."

She growled. "She's in your dreams?"

"Making all the things I worry about come to fruition," he whispered, nuzzling back into her neck.

She hurt for him because she now knew how much he worried about his little sister. That his grandmother would use that weakness against him was low. She went through protection spells that she'd tried using for Israel when she wanted to keep him from her dreams. She hadn't found any that worked, but it wouldn't stop her from attempting for his sake.

He chuckled into her neck. "I can almost hear you thinking."

"I'm going to find a way to block her from your dreams."

"Oh yeah?" He gripped her chin with his fingers. His eyes held amusement, but heat was there in their dark depths. "You're gonna save me, kitty cat?"

She smiled, happy that she'd been able to bring him out of the funk she knew his nightmares often put him in. Israel kissed her, a soft touch of lips that broadcasted his relief. It wasn't long before he deepened the kiss, his tongue lazily tangling with hers. He grew stiff beneath her, shifting her hips until his dick was nestled right at the center of her. She'd gone to sleep with no panties on, and she thanked her past self for that.

She sighed when he slid inside her, rocking her hips to take him fully. She guessed that he wouldn't have any more nightmares if they didn't sleep. Look at her already doing her part to help.

Chapter Twenty-Three

Audrey was nervous. But that was expected. It wasn't every day that she stole something from a museum in the middle of a crowded gala. She fidgeted in the expensive gown that her Aunt Lauren had insisted she wear for the occasion. The emerald green dress fit her like second skin. The front was high, skimming her collar bone, the back plunging nearly to the top of her ass. From the way Israel's eyes had dropped into slits, he really liked it.

He licked his lips and walked a lap around her. The heat from his stare warmed her body and beaded her nipples. He slid a hand down her back, and she sucked in a breath, turned on.

"You look exquisite," he murmured in her ear.

The heated press of his body behind her had her clit throbbing in need. Israel dropped soft kisses on her shoulder.

"I'm ripping this off you the very moment we're done." He promised in a dark voice.

"So, in the car on the way home?" she husked out.

Israel bent her over the desk in their hotel room, smacking her ass before crowding her. "The very fucking second."

Audrey bit back a moan and stood straight. She turned around and adjusted the bow tie at his throat, her hands shaking in arousal.

"You need to concentrate," she murmured.

He closed his eyes and breathed deep. "You're right. But goddamn woman, you got my head fucked up." His dark eyes were intense, nearly black, as he opened them, spearing her with a desperate look.

She swallowed and stepped back. "If it all goes to plan, this won't take long. You'll have me soon enough."

He nodded and walked to the other side of the room. He came back with a green plastic sheet dangling from his fingers. Audrey frowned.

"I need you to wear this."

She chuckled. "You playing. I ain't covering this bomb ass dress."

"Trust me, kitten," he said, draping it over her shoulders.

She sucked her teeth but gasped when the plastic changed into a flowing cape. Crystals encrusted it, and it matched her dress.

"Your magic is amazing," she told him. He looked sheepish, and she could feel his embarrassment. She cupped his cheek, "I imagined if you were lighter, you'd be blushing."

He kissed her. "You're distracting," he murmured against her lips. "Now come on. We got some stealing to do."

Butterflies attacked her stomach, and her cat moved through her body. Israel rubbed a hand down her back, and the animal settled. Audrey smiled at him in relief. The last thing she needed was her magic flaring out of control.

"I'm ready," she told him.

The ride over to the museum was silent, tense. Usually, she'd try to fill it in with chatter, but she was too nervous. She hadn't been to Savannah in some years, so she took in the scenery to try and calm her nerves. Audrey gasped and looked at her husband as the limo pulled up to the valet directly outside the brick building. There was a crush of people waiting to get in. The official opening wasn't supposed to be until tomorrow.

"I thought this was supposed to be the first look?"

His shoulders straightened, a determined look covering his face. "The crowd might make it a little easier."

The window between them and the driver came down. "I'll be waiting with the car running, Lucky. " Eli told them. "I'm glad we sent the twins back to Miami. We've always been able to move better with just the two of us."

Israel chuckled.

Audrey sucked her teeth. "I can't imagine what the two of you get into."

Israel kissed her lips. "Showtime, kitty cat."

She nodded. She scanned the crowd as Israel came around to open her door. She didn't recognize any of the faces in the crowd. Israel grabbed her hand, and she squeezed him, letting him know she was good. He handed the guard at the door their invitation, and they entered the beautiful event.

The inside was like any other museum she'd visited. They passed the gift shop, walking until they reached an arch that read 'Savannah's Black History.' She was impressed with it all. All eyes went to them as they entered the space. Even with Israel's at her side, she felt a little self-conscious.

"Why is everyone looking at us?" She whispered.

"The cape. Between you in that dress and the enchantment on the cape, no one will notice me at your side," he told her, patting her hand.

He said it so nonchalantly. She took a deep, shuddering breath. His magic was some potent shit.

No pressure.

Israel spotted his grandmother and aunt, and they both turned to him as though summoned. Annabelle's greedy gaze raked over Audrey, and for a moment, worry tried to break through his confident façade. He tucked Audrey's hand into his elbow.

"Do not leave my side," he reminded her.

Her nervousness was tucked firmly behind the shield over her mind. The confident woman that he knew and loved was back in place.

"I know the drill." She turned to him and fixed his lapels, smoothing her hand down his chest. "Relax, we got this. Now, show me your family."

He nodded and walked her around the Deleon exhibit. There were pictures and letters behind a glass wall, their descriptions below. The lighting was brighter than he'd anticipated, but it gave him the opportunity to study the pictures of his family, going back as far as the eighteen hundreds. He got nostalgic seeing the items from his grandfather and stuff that his father had shown to him. He didn't get a lot of years with his father, but he loved him and remembered him fondly.

He stopped in front of the large framed painting of his grandfather Darren and could almost smell the leather and tobacco smell that was intrinsic to him. Darren stared down his nose at observers, the power in his gaze no less intimidating even on canvas. His grandfather had been powerful, though he'd only used his magic to tend to his farm and keep his wife out of trouble. Or at least he'd tried. Darren had died when Israel was maybe ten. Annabelle hadn't taken it well, and the tyrant Israel knew her to be was born after his death.

Audrey gripped his hand. "Are you okay?"

He nodded, swallowing down the lump in his throat. He had a mission and wouldn't let memories weigh him down. He put his focus back where it belonged and finally spotted the almanac. Before he could head that way, his grandmother sidled up to them.

He sighed. "Annabelle, you remember my wife, Audrey."

Annabelle gave them a cold smile. "Of course, the little Fouche."

Audrey stiffened at his side. He didn't have to probe her mind to feel the aggravation filling her. But before they could say anything, raised voices carried to them. Annabelle turned, and her eyes narrowed as she got a look at who was causing the noise.

Audrey's family had finally arrived.

"What are they doing here?" Annabelle hissed.

She left him and Audrey alone, storming over to the Fouche's. Audrey released a relieved breath, and the two of them headed towards the almanac with determined steps.

He took a drink and a few napkins off a tray from a waiter as he passed. Audrey raised her eye at the number of napkins as she accepted the wine glass from him. Her curiosity pressed against him, but he blocked it out, focused on the task at hand.

"Will your family be able to pull it off?" He asked absently.

She snorted and took a sip of her wine. "Trust me. Aunt Dawn and Aunt Lauren can show their asses at the drop of a dime."

"Watch my back then," he murmured, turning to the almanac on display.

It was on a wooden podium, nothing between it and the party goers. That made his job that much easier. He was mindful of how much magic he used, not wanting to bring any attention to his actions. Between Audrey's cape and the natural magic that swirled around her, he hoped that the use of his power would go unnoticed. He rubbed his hands together and murmured the spell he'd prepared ahead of time. He'd wondered if Audrey's magic being bonded to his would change his in any way. As his spell went up, he could feel the difference in its power.

Very interesting.

He would have to examine that later. Once he was finished, he flipped the almanac to the back pages. They were blank, just as Jacob had written. Israel gently ripped the last two blank pages out of the almanac. He placed the napkins in their place, and with a few gentle massages from his finger, and the weaving of his spell over them, the napkins changed to match the other pages. He pulled his magic back and turned at Audrey's soft gasp.

Her eyes were wide as she stared at the book and then back at him. "Holy shit."

He smiled, and they moved away from the exhibit. The commotion had quieted, and a sense of triumph filled him. Now they only had to get out of the museum alive.

Audrey stared at her husband as he gently folded the pages he'd ripped from his great-grandfather's book. Israel's eyes scanned the crowd to ensure they hadn't been seen. She was amazed by his power. She looked back at the almanac, which looked just as it had before. No trace of his magic was left to hint that something had happened. Israel guided them into a corner, and he pulled out the pages. She looked down into his hands. Why in the world would he take blank pages?

"That's what this is all about? A couple of blank pages?"

He chuckled and stepped closer to her. He lifted a single finger, traced something along her forehead, and kissed it. Her head tingled, and she looked up to meet his gaze. He leaned down and captured her mouth in a soul-stirring kiss. She was breathless when he finished, the room falling into the shadows. They stared at each other a few beats longer, the space charged with tension.

Someone bumped into her, and it broke up their moment, the crowd's noise registering again. Audrey looked around, and her eyes widened. There was magic in the air, floating around some of the Deleon artifacts. Her heart started racing, and she turned back to Israel.

"Is that how you see?"

He nodded. "When I have my magic up, yes." He dipped his chin down towards the pages.

Her breath caught at the scrawled writing covering the pages that had been blank only a second ago.

"Oh my God," she whispered.

"Exactly," Israel said, tucking the pages into his jacket pocket. "It's time to go."

She nodded and followed him through the crowd. They were stopped at the door by security.

"Sir, I'll have to check your pockets."

"You can't be serious," Israel said.

His demeanor was calm, unlike Audrey's, whose heart was beating a million beats a minute. She gave a panicked look around until she spotted her Aunt Lauren. Her Aunt winked at her, and Audrey turned back to the security guard. He reached into Israel's jacket pocket, and for a moment, she thought she would faint. Instead of the pages she'd witnessed Israel stuff into his pocket, the security guard pulled out napkins.

"Are the napkins that valuable?" Israel asked.

His tone made the guard flush in embarrassment. Before the man could answer, there was a scream, and Audrey turned to witness her Aunt Dawn splayed on the floor. Lauren was loudly fawning over her sister, asking for a doctor. Israel snatched the napkins from the guard, and he and Audrey hauled ass out of the venue. She tapped her foot as they waited for Eli to bring the limo around to them. She didn't breathe a sigh of relief until they slid into the back seat.

Adrenaline had Audrey giggling. "I can't believe we did that."

"Believe it," he said, laying his head back onto the seat. "We got one more stop before the night is over."

Chapter Twenty-Four

Israel's heart was racing with their close call. Audrey's face was suffused with warmth, her smile filling him with an almost savage need for her. Now that they'd gotten away with it, his adrenaline was being channeled entirely into lust. He pressed the button next to him to raise the partition between them and Eli. He could've hired a driver for the occasion, but he didn't entrust his or Audrey's safety to anyone outside of his team, especially on his grandmother's home turf.

Audrey gave him a startled look once the partition was closed.

"Come to me, kitten." His heart was thumping hard, sending lust through his bloodstream.

She slid closer to him on the seat, and he grabbed her around the waist, tugging her into his lap.

He nuzzled into her neck, his teeth scraping down her neck. "Do you have any idea how hot you look?" He used the sharp point of his ring to slice down the seam of the skirt of her dress.

"Lucky! I liked this dress," she protested.

"Everyone else in the room paled compared to you," he whispered, ignoring her protest.

He grabbed her chin and brought her face closer to his. She gasped, and he used that opportunity to push his tongue into her mouth. It only took a millisecond for her to return his kiss. She gripped the sides of his face and tilted her head, their tongues dueling. She moaned and pulled back.

"Lucky, you don't want to wait until we get back to the hotel?" The mischievous smile on her face lit a fire in him.

He loved this playful side to her.

He slid his hand up her thigh, cupping her pussy. It was wet, the heat coming from it making him salivate for a taste. "How long did you think I could resist you in this dress, kitty cat?"

Her eyes went slumberous, her breath hitching. "We'll be there soon."

"What did I tell you earlier?" He dragged kisses along the back of her neck.

He could see her heartbeat thumping against her neck, speeding up as he slid his fingers into her barely there panties. He traced a line down her slit.

"Lucky," she whispered.

"Yes, love?" He asked, bringing her mouth to him for another kiss.

He inserted a finger when he inserted his tongue into her mouth. Both digits moved with the same motion. She squirmed in his lap, and he couldn't help the moan that slipped from him. She was warm, wet and his dick throbbed in anticipation. She whimpered as his thumb caressed her clit. She released his lips, and her head fell back on a lustful sigh.

"Lucky," she moaned again, this time in need.

"I want you, here, now. Say yes, kitten."

Her forehead lowered against his. "Yes."

He growled and lifted her until she straddled him, her dress bunched around her hips. He impatiently snapped her thong as she worked on the zipper of his slacks. She mewled, guiding her scorching pussy over his dick. The first slide down had him seeing stars. He had to take a deep breath and calm himself because he was seconds from powering into her and fucking her until neither of them could walk.

Possessive need rose in him, the need to mark her overwhelming him. She was his, and he would do anything to prove it to her. Audrey dragged her teeth across his skin before biting his neck. His hips bucked, and she chuckled. She rose slowly, her walls dragging along his dick tortuously.

"You minx," he murmured, pulling back down, impaling her with his erection.

She gasped, her breath brushing against his neck.

"Ride, kitten," He ordered, leaning back on the seat.

She leaned back, and the heated look she gave him was his undoing. How could he not be in love with this woman? Audrey followed his demands, her hips working on top of him. She was a beautiful, breathtaking sight. This time in the limousine had to be quick, he understood that, but God damn this woman, he wanted to stay inside her all night.

She laughed, in his mind as always. "We got shit to do." She reminded him.

He grabbed her hips and lurched up, driving deep within her. "Take this nut then, kitty cat."

Her walls clenched around him, and Israel cursed, his toes curling with pleasure. She scraped her nails down the back of his neck and leaned forward, taking his mouth in a deep kiss as she moaned. He brushed his thumb over her clit, and she jerked, swirling her hips on top of him, chasing her own orgasm.

"Now, Lucky," she demanded, rocking her hips and squeezing down on him.

He obeyed, crying out into her mouth. Pleasure washed over him, goosebumps rising on his arms as he came. Audrey pulled back, panting for air, biting her bottom lip as she tipped over the edge. Her orgasm had her pulsing around his dick, prolonging his own. He buried his face in her neck, breathing in her scent, basking in the magic that swirled around them.

"I don't know that I'm gonna be up for any more shenanigans tonight," she murmured, snuggling into his chest.

He chuckled as she nuzzled her cheek against him. He'd missed her like this most of all. A satiated kitten that curled into him after they had sex.

"I don't know why you keep acting like you don't know why we call you kitty cat," he told her as she nestled closer, damn near purring in his arms.

She laughed lazily, rubbing her face against his neck, inhaling deep. "Hey, I should be able to cuddle with my husband without earning a nickname."

He laughed, happy to have her back in his arms.

Chapter Twenty-Five

Israel lazily raked the towel over the top of his head as he leaned over the desk in their hotel room. He was reading through the last page of Jacob's Almanac to confirm where they were headed. He'd read the passage in the museum, but it had been at a glance, and he wanted to make certain he had it right. Where they were headed was dangerous, so he couldn't afford a mistake. He stood straight as he heard Audrey's family moving down the hotel hallway.

Eli escorted them into his room, a smirk on his best friend's face. He could only imagine what he'd overheard from the women. They were playfully arguing about who gave the best performance as they entered his room. He raised an eyebrow because the women were supposed to be on their way back to Springbrook. Eli just shrugged.

"Ladies," Israel greeted them as they crowded into the room. "You were amazing."

"Of course," Lauren said, waving her hand. "We just wanted to check and make sure you two made it safely before we headed out. We left Shelby and Kit in the car."

He nodded. "We have another stop before we can leave Savannah."

"Did you get what you needed from the gala?" Dawn asked.

"Yes, ma'am."

Lauren snorted and hugged him. "Playing nice, huh?"

He was touched by the warmth he felt from Nicole's mother. Dawn hugged him next, and the two of them headed towards the door.

"Be careful, nephew. We'll see you two when you get home." Dawn called out.

Home.

He was struck speechless. He could only nod at the women as they left. They welcomed him just on the strength of his marriage to Audrey. Had he ever had acceptance that he didn't have to fight for tooth and nail? Under the brutal power of his magic was the only time he'd ever been able to demand a place in the world. It was stunning to get it so freely from his wife's family. He was gathering the materials they needed for the night, still stunned when Audrey stepped from the bathroom.

"Did I hear my aunts out here?" She asked.

She wore simple black leggings and a black hoodie, covering damn near every part of her skin, and yet he bricked up as though she'd walked out naked. She was so damn beautiful.

"You ready," he managed to choke out.

"What's wrong?" She gripped his chin, her fingers tugging the hair of his beard, and forced his gaze to meet hers.

"Just mentally preparing for the next step."

She studied him a moment before she let him go. He could see in her eyes that she didn't quite believe him, but she let it drop.

"Where are we headed?"

"We're going grave robbing."

"Oh lord," she muttered.

She didn't say anything else, simply gathering her bag. No hysterics, no million questions. That shouldn't turn him on, but it did. A woman who was down for whatever was a novelty for him, and he was finding out that he liked it very much. It forced him to take another look at how he'd treated their marriage before. He hid so much from his wife, which all seemed especially unnecessary in light of how she'd handled herself tonight. He'd been opening up to her more every day, and she'd proven to him that she could handle his lifestyle at every turn. He could've ruined it all had he let his grandmother continue to control him.

It strengthened his resolve.

He would break his family's curse over Audrey's and remove himself from under Annabelle's thumb, no matter what. He straightened his shoulders and took a deep breath to get his mind right. They had a cemetery to break into.

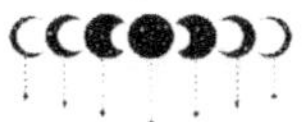

"Nah, I need you to run that back to me," Eli said as he guided the SUV down the dark road towards Israel's family's burial plot.

It wasn't in any old cemetery. The Deleon's had their own, hidden away from prying eyes. It wasn't on his grandmother's property which was a saving grace for them. Israel said Annabelle would know immediately if they were on her land. It would still be pushing it with the cemetery, but if their luck held, his grandmother wouldn't know anything until they were well on their way back to Springbrook.

"All you need to do is stay in the car with it running," Israel said, grabbing items out of his bag.

Audrey shuddered. "I can feel the protection and power here."

"You're safe enough with me," Israel told her. He grabbed her chin and kissed her.

"You should let me go with you, Lucky." Eli turned to the back seat to watch his best friend.

Audrey lowkey agreed, but she would trust that Israel knew what he was doing. They'd gotten out of the museum just as he said they would. She could extend that trust a little further.

"What's in the bag?" She asked.

"Contingency plans," he told them. "We may come out of there hot, Eli, so be ready to ride the moment we get in the truck."

Eli sighed but nodded his assent.

Audrey got out of the car and shivered at the damp air surrounding the cemetery. It was a small one, maybe only twenty or so headstones. Beyond the headstones was a large mausoleum that stood tall and forbidden. She wondered how many of Israel's dead relatives were housed within. They must have been important to be separated from the other graves.

A metal fence surrounded the whole plot, but it was the invisible line of power that more than likely kept out intruders. Israel walked ahead of her to the main gate. It had the Deleon name in metal letters across the entrance.

Israel dropped his bag carefully to the ground and reached inside. Audrey frowned when he pulled out a tuning fork. He touched it to the gate, and it started to vibrate a haunting note that sent chills down her spine. He closed his eyes, touched it again, and this time the tinny noise was slightly higher. He murmured under his breath, and Audrey felt him gathering magic. The tuning fork vibrated at a lower note, the note louder with every pull of Israel's magic until her ears popped. Once that happened, the ground started to shake within the gates.

Audrey released her magic and switched her vision to see what kind of spell work was around. She watched as the spell protecting the cemetery from intruders dissipated in a burst of colors. Unfortunately, she also noticed the ghouls starting to rise from the ground.

She cursed and blinked her eyes to go back to her normal vision. She wracked her mind for something to do. Luckily for her, her family passed superstitions around like bedtime stories. She knew one way to help. Audrey bent down to the ground and reached her hands between the bars of the gate.

"What are you doing?" Israel asked.

She handed him a hand full of the dirt. "Rub this on your pulse points, quickly." She showed him which scent points to hit.

He didn't ask any further questions, just followed her instructions. He looked up and cursed when he noticed the ghouls. They were already disoriented. "Good call."

She nodded. "Where ever we have to go, walk carefully, but quickly. The dirt will only confuse them but for so long."

Israel carefully opened the gate, and they slipped in. He walked quickly towards the mausoleum at the back of the graveyard. She swallowed a scream when one of the ghouls reached for them but missed. She breathed slightly easier once they reached their destination. The mausoleum was cold, the stone damp, the earthy smell making her crinkle her nose. Israel circled the large columns, and Audrey counted four doors with names and dates etched into them. She wondered at their standing in the Deleon family that they had been buried with such distinction.

They finally rounded the back, losing sight of the rest of the graveyard. Israel reached into his bag and pulled out chalk this time. He wrote on the stone door, his voice low and forceful as he completed the spell. A quiet snick sounded, and a dusty, musky smell of old cloth and bones wafted from the opening. Israel stuck his hand in and reached around for what felt like the longest seconds of her life. He grunted and pulled out a worn sack.

"Got it. Let's go."

Audrey shuddered again as they made their way back to the car. The ghouls wandering around had doubled while they'd been out of sight. The gate was in view, so they hastened their steps. She lost track of where she was stepping, and the heel of her foot hit the corner of a grave. Before she could snatch her foot away, a grave hag gripped her ankle and pulled. Audrey wobbled, nearly falling before Israel caught her in his arms. She used her other foot to stomp on the hand holding onto her ankle, scrambling away the moment she was free.

She cursed as the grave hag sprang up and lurched towards them. She lifted her hand to throw up a spell, but Israel beat her to it, stunning the creature.

"Run," he prodded her.

She took off, careful not to step on any of the graves and trigger any other defensive spells his family had set out to trap trespassers. The sweat from their run was washing away the dirt, and the ghouls were now wholly focused on them, picking up their scent. By the time they were close to the gate, she was breathless, her strength depleting with every spell she threw. Israel cursed next to her and stopped.

"Keep going!" He shouted at her. "Stay!" He ordered Eli, who had left the car, and raced towards them.

"Not without you," she gritted out, pulling more magic from the air around them. She stood at his side, her shoulders back, ready for whatever.

He growled but said nothing else, his hands moving in a complicated pattern. Electricity crackled around him, and the hair on her arms stood straight. Israel clapped his hands together once before making a pulling down motion. Lightning struck the graveyard. A sharp, bright bolt hit the grave hag first before taking down the ghouls. The smell of burning flesh stung her nose, the screaming ghouls turning her stomach. The light of the lightning momentarily blinded her, and she was thankful that she didn't have to watch the creatures burn.

Moments later, silence descended, and only smoke was left of the creatures.

"We'll talk about this when we're safely home," Israel gritted out —tugging her into his arms.

"There's nothing to talk about as far as I'm concerned." She pushed from him and headed for the gate.

She could feel the difference once she crossed back through the gates. The heavy press of magic lightened, and she could finally breathe easier.

Eli paced outside of the SUV.

"Don't start, Eli. We're fine." Israel said tiredly as his friend opened his mouth. "Into the truck, kitten."

Audrey did as he ordered, grateful to be within the safe confines of the car.

"Your family doesn't fuck around." She said, winded.

"Not one bit," he muttered. "Let's ride, Eli. We gotta get out of my grandmother's territory before she finds out what's happened."

Israel didn't follow her into the car. Instead, he turned her body so her legs dangled out of the SUV. He slid between them, rubbing his cheek against hers. He lifted his head a second later, and she tensed, expecting a lecture for not leaving him.

As if she would.

She didn't know what other kinds of people Israel dealt with, but now that she was in this marriage, she was riding with him. His jaw flexed, and the turmoil in his mind was reflected on his face.

"You smell like graveyard dirt." He finally said.

She laughed and let out a relieved breath. She hugged him tightly. "You say the sweetest things."

Chapter Twenty Six

Israel was exhausted. The ride from Savannah to Springbrook was an hour long. That hour after what they'd just done felt like six. He was highly appreciative of Eli. His best friend was steady on the dark highway. Audrey slept in the back seat, her beautiful face relaxed. He'd been tempted to stay back there with her, but he hadn't wanted Eli in the front alone this late at night. Israel was still alert. Though they'd left his grandmother's territory, he wouldn't put anything past Annabelle. He'd relaxed once they got closer to Fouche land.

He turned back to gaze at Audrey, as always, fascinated with her. Eli chuckled next to him in the driver's seat.

"You and that woman, man."

Israel snorted. "I don't know what it is, Eli. It's damn near obsession."

"Damn near?" Eli chuckled quietly. "What are you going to do, Lucky? You think it will be easy to convince her to leave her cousins?"

Israel sighed. That was his current debate. He had business in Miami, but nothing said he couldn't work from anywhere. He could set up his office in any city. He had offices just south of Georgia in Jacksonville. Nothing was stopping him from setting up there if he wanted a little distance from the Fouche's. He'd hustled his way to the top of Miami in a year; Jacksonville would be no different. Well...there would be some difference. He imagined his wife wouldn't let him do the things he needed to get the job done quickly. She would more than likely curb some of his more violent tactics.

He sighed and put his eyes back on the road. There was little to no traffic on the highway. Being that it was close to four am, he wasn't surprised. They pulled off onto the Springbrook exit, and he breathed a sigh of relief. He was ready to crash. He frowned when they finally pulled up to the Fouche house. The lights were on.

"Lord, it's always something going on here," Eli grumbled. "I'll be happy to go home just to get uninterrupted sleep."

Israel snorted. The women did always have something going on. He got out of the car and stretched before walking around to the other side and opening the door. He gently scooped his wife into his arms. He cuddled her close, happy that she was with him. She snuggled into his neck and sighed.

"I can't wait to get in bed," she mumbled.

"A shower, and then we can sleep, kitten." He kissed the top of her hair.

Her head popped up, and she frowned. "Let me down, Iz." She looked at the house before looking back at him. "Something's wrong."

"You can tell that from just looking at the house?" Eli asked.

"The energy feels off," she muttered, rushing up the steps to the front door.

He was right behind her, nearly slamming into her back as she abruptly stopped. Nic and Ness shot her worried looks as she came in. They looked behind them expectantly.

"The moms aren't with you?" Nic asked. Worry coated her face.

"What do you mean? We sent them back hours ahead of us." Audrey turned back to look at him.

Ness stood from the sofa and rushed to the window. "They haven't arrived, and they're not answering their phones."

Israel got nervous, though he couldn't tell if it were his own feelings or his wife's flowing down their bond.

"Do you think your grandmother got to them?" Audrey asked him.

"If she has them, then we have a little time because she hasn't called to taunt me about it." He told her grimly.

"Y'all are doing that telepathic talking thing," Ness said, narrowing her eyes. "Should we wait a little longer?"

Audrey closed her eyes, and Israel could feel the swell of her power. "I still feel mama, so where ever they are, they're alive."

"Thank God," Nic said, slumping on the sofa.

"Did either of you get any sleep?" Israel asked them.

They both shook their heads.

"We should've gone with them," Nic murmured.

"Your power broadcasts very loudly, Nicole," Israel told her. "Had you stepped one foot onto my grandmother's territory, we would've had a whole new problem."

"What y'all wanna do?" Eli asked.

Israel looked around at their exhausted faces. "I know it will be hard, but we can't think while tired. Let's try and get a couple of hours of sleep. We can get up and start looking after that."

The women nodded reluctantly. When he thought they'd disperse for upstairs, they instead started building pallets from the blankets and pillows they got from a hallway closet.

He grabbed his wife around the waist. *"You sleeping in here?"*

"My cousins need me." She said.

He nodded and kissed her forehead. *"Do you need me?"*

She cupped his cheek, her eyes full of love. It filled his heart and their bond. *"It's a cousin thing. Go rest."*

His gaze traced her face, almost as though he wanted to memorize her features before he went to sleep. With a final light kiss, he went upstairs to try and get some sleep. He had a feeling that Audrey was right and his grandmother had the Fouche women. But like he told her. Annabelle couldn't resist taunting him. If nothing else, that would buy them some time.

Israel cursed as his phone vibrated across the bedside table. He squinted at the display, sitting up as he realized it was a video call.

"Yeah," he managed to croak out.

"Lucky," His Aunt Sabine was whispering, her eyes desperate.

Israel slid from beneath the sheet and sat on the edge of the bed, shaking the sleep from his head. "What's wrong?"

"She has Arianne. You need to come back."

"Has her where? What's happened?"

Tears crested his aunt's eyes before their slow descent down her cheeks. "I tried to stop her, Lucky. She's going to perform the—"

The call dropped, but it didn't matter. Israel was already getting dressed. He summoned Eli to him and rushed down the stairs to wake his wife. The women were still sleeping in the living room, but Audrey seemed to sense him, waking immediately. She stood from her pallet and rushed to him.

"What's wrong?"

"My grandmother is using my sister for the ceremony."

"Give me five minutes. Just five, Iz," she rushed from him up the stairs before he could agree or disagree.

Ness was the next one up. She sat up, rubbing her eyes. "What's going on?"

He didn't feel like explaining. He wanted to be on the road. Grief, worry, and he hated to admit it, but fear was strangling his voice. She stared at him a moment before nodding. She shook Nicole awake.

"Up, we need to ride. Call JT and them." She got up from the sofa and turned to Israel. "Let me brush my teeth and wash my face, and I'll be ready."

A groggy Nicole was mumbling on her phone, but she moved purposefully.

Just like that, no questions. It baffled him because he was only used to those he controlled having his back that way.

Eli rushed down the stairs. "I'll get the car ready."

He stopped next to Israel and gripped the back of his neck. Eli's lion moved through Israel, feeding his magic and giving him support. Even before he'd realized he had an animal to call, Israel and Eli had been as close as brothers. Magic strengthened a bond that had already been forged to the point where either of them could give the other power. Israel was deeply appreciative of it now. The boost helped him push away most of the fear that had him rooted to the floor.

He closed his eyes and sighed, pushing past his panic to plan. If Annabelle was preparing a ritual, then that meant she had a practitioner. It was too much of a coincidence that Audrey's mother and aunts were missing. They needed to hurry if that were the case. He turned to yell for the women, but the three rushed downstairs, all in black jogging suits, with knit caps covering their hair. That gave him pause because what in the world had these three been getting into that they could be ready at a moment's notice.

This family continued to intrigue him.

"You've met our mothers. We stay ready for bullshit," Audrey told him, reading his thoughts easily. She gripped his hand. "Let's go."

They rushed out to the truck. He was helping them into the back seat when he heard the motorcycles.

"They're meeting us at the highway," Nic told him, jumping into the backseat.

Just like that, then.

At that moment, Israel understood that he would be making life changes. He couldn't possibly take all of this from his wife. That was a problem for another day, though. Right now, he needed to rescue his sister.

Israel climbed into the front seat.

"I take it we have back-up?" Eli asked, starting the car.

Israel nodded. "Seems so."

As soon as they hit the highway, a line of motorcycles and trucks sidled up behind them. They were officially an entourage. Israel tried calling Sabine again, cursing when the phone went straight to voicemail. Eli pressed his foot down on the gas without prompting, sensing Israel's frustration.

"What happened, Lucky?" Audrey sat forward to ask.

"Aunt Sabine called. Said my grandmother had Arianne and was planning the ritual."

She gasped. "The same ritual that drains practitioners?"

He nodded and tried to call his aunt again.

"Fuck," she whispered. "She has the moms."

"Wait, what?" Nic asked.

"It's too long to explain—"

"—we have an hour," Ness cut in.

Israel sighed. "Right. You're right. I think my grandmother has your mothers and plans to use a ritual my family has used to drain them of their power."

"Hey, lion. Make this shit go faster," Ness ordered.

If they were lucky, Eli could cut that hour in half.

Chapter Twenty Seven

Audrey was nervous, and her head hurt from lack of sleep and the worry she could feel from Israel down their bond. The closer to Savannah they got, the more that anxiety morphed into anger. It was beating along their connection, his magic swelling in the car. She reached and grabbed his shoulder.

"Pull it back a bit, my love. You're drowning us."

He didn't respond, but the pressure in the car lightened.

"Thank God," Ness murmured. "Good luck trying to tame all that magic, cuzzo."

Audrey snorted. She had no desire to tame her husband. She loved all that raw power. They rode the rest of the way in silence. Nicole was communicating with the Taylors, her fingers moving quickly over her phone's keyboard. She looked behind them and frowned when the wolf pack got off at an exit without them.

She turned her attention to Nic. "What's wrong?"

"JT had to get permission to pass through the territory with so many of them. They'll catch up." Nic reassured her.

Finally, after an hour on the road, they turned off at an exit. There were no gas stations or restaurants at this exit. It was all wooded area, with two lanes in and out. She was surprised that it warranted an actual exit from the highway. Even though it was nearing noon, the sun struggled to reach through those trees. Audrey squinted as they approached what looked like a dead end. There was a big no trespassing sign in front of the heavily wooded area where the road ended. Were they going through there? She didn't see how.

"Ahh shit," Ness murmured.

Audrey cosigned that sentiment. It felt oppressive as hell. Something in her wanted her to turn around, but she could feel her mother just on the edge of her consciousness.

"They're here," she whispered.

Nic nodded. "I feel mama, too."

"Along with some crazy shit," Ness told them.

Audrey understood what she meant. If his grandmother's magic reached all the way to the exit, then what were they in store for? Eli pulled the truck over, and she was curious until she heard the sound of JT and his gang coming up. Before they could pull over, Eli pulled out in front of them, and they continued their convoy. Eli turned to the left right before they reached the sign, a small road she didn't imagine anyone would even think to look for. Soon, they got to another turnoff, a metal gate protecting it. The metal gate had the same etching and initials as the cometary they raided last night. She shuddered.

Israel opened his car door. "Drive when I order you to."

Eli nodded in agreement. Israel got out and walked back to JT. She turned in her seat to watch him, curious when JT nodded. Audrey turned her attention back to the gate, flaring her magic to see past the façade of trees and shrubbery. A ward shimmered bright, pearlescent like the inside of a seashell. It was opaque and thicker than the wards around the Fouche property. She was intrigued. Could she use her magic to take it down?

"*Don't, love,*" Israel ordered. He was a shadow in her mind.

She sucked her teeth and waited for him to do what he was going to do. She didn't pull back her magic, though. For one, she wanted to see what he would do, and for two, she wanted to make sure she was there for backup if he needed it. Israel's hands moved in small movements as he traced out runes, placing them around the gate. With her magic up, she could see every placement. With the last one, a sliver of the ward opened, slowly widening as Israel widened his hands. She didn't hear Israel speak aloud, but Eli started driving. She held her breath as they approached the ward. It didn't look big enough for them to fit through, but they did. JT and his crew were behind them. She looked ahead, curious to know what they were stumbling into.

The heavy weight of the magic pressed against her skin, making the hair on the back of her neck stand up.

"Fuck," Ness said next to her. "This doesn't have the light feel of Grandmother's magic."

"Ain't shit light about Annabelle Deleon," Eli told them.

Ness and Nic cursed next to her, and she focused her attention in front of the car. It was a plantation, a huge one. The white columns ascended from the ground up to the second-floor roof. Two spiral stairs led to the second-floor balcony. The house was pristine as though it hadn't been touched by the passing time. But the magic and aura coming to the place were centuries old. The lush landscaping in the front belied its spooky feeling.

It was as if two different entities resided in the house.

Audrey shuddered. There was a stone fountain in the front, the circular drive surrounding it. Eli stopped at the beginning of the driveway, and they piled out of the car.

"Where do we start?" Audrey asked.

"She knows we're here," Israel said grimly as he walked up to them.

No sooner than he said that did the woods surrounding the property get wild. Big cats from every species poured from the woods in their animal form and headed their way. Audrey knew that cats were Israel's animal to call, but with so many...

She turned to him, worried. "I can feel my aunts and a shit ton of magic. Your grandmother's doing something."

"I can feel it too. I can probably gain control of them," Israel told them.

"You'll lose too much time. Go," Ness ordered the two of them.

JT hopped off his motorcycle. "Fouche!" He called out to his mate.

"I'm on it, baby." Nicole started chanting.

Audrey felt the press of heat from the wolves' magic as they shifted and prepared themselves. The ground started shaking, and the approaching cats started tripping as Nic dragged up tree roots.

"Go, we'll take this," Ness insisted.

Israel raced towards the back with Eli and Audrey on his heels. Her husband was preparing for the worst, yet Audrey still was not ready for what they saw when they circled the back of the house. Between two small huts, that she knew from the look used to be slave quarters, was a raging fire. On one side of the fire, her mother and three aunts were tied together.

They could make out a young girl on the other side of the fire, but she was kneeling on the ground over a prone body. Israel cursed this time.

"My aunt." He answered her unspoken question.

She didn't know what she had been expecting, but her mother and aunts tied in the middle of a power circle was not it. Israel's grandmother stepped from behind the fire, and her white cotton dress swept the ground. Her long gray locks flowed loosely down her back, the coarse strands blowing in the wind. Annabelle's voice carried strong as she started an incantation.

Chapter Twenty-Eight

He'd felt the magic the moment they'd gotten through the ward of Annabelle's property, but he still couldn't believe what she was doing. Israel's stomach turned as he recognized the words from the incantation his grandmother was chanting. He blinked, flipping to his inner eye. He could see the parasitic strings of magic floating around Audrey's family. The further along the ceremony went, the thicker those strings would get until they bound the women tightly, leaving them helpless. Indecision gripped him for a moment. His aunt was on the ground, hopefully just unconscious. He wanted to save her, but stopping Annabelle had to take precedence.

Dealing with the fallout if he allowed his grandmother to finish would endanger so many more people. If she completed the ritual and got a hold of the Fouche's power, stopping her would be near impossible. As it was, Annabelle was already at the top of her power here on her territory.

"Eli," he said.

"I got it," Eli assured him, shifting immediately.

Words weren't needed. With the bond he had with his best

friend, Eli already knew what he needed. He darted off to their right in his lion form, disappearing into the darkening forest.

Annabelle looked up and finally noticed him and Audrey. His grandmother's smile was sinister as she snatched a crying Arianne up. She held the point of her dagger to his sister's neck, all while continuing her chant. Fear spiked for Israel, and for a moment, he was paralyzed. There was no more time to decide. He needed to make a decision.

"I don't recognize that incantation," Audrey whispered. "What are our options?"

Fuck if he knew. "It's a vas ritual. She's trying to replace me with my sister."

"And use my mother's power as a sacrifice? Fuck that," Audrey said.

Her magic swelled as she immediately went to work. He didn't have time to wonder what she was doing. His mind was spinning. The goddess Kisasi's body was wavering as Annabelle continued the incantation, her presence almost solidifying. Israel knew the words by heart and knew that Annabelle was coming up to a pause where she had to wait on the gateway to open completely.

They were running out of time.

Annabelle smiled triumphantly as she stopped chanting. "I thought you would be happy, Israel. You get to keep your wife, and I will soon replace you as the family vas."

"Arianne is too young to handle the power," Israel yelled over the whipping magic. "I won't let you do this."

"I have doubled the offering to the goddess. Do you imagine she will turn it down?" Annabelle scoffed. "Arrogant boy."

"You aren't the family vas." The goddess' voice was still far away, echoing around the night air. Kisasi's body wavered, ephemeral as her presence made its way through the open gateway of her world.

"I offer a replacement," Annabelle called out and tossed Arianne down at the goddess' feet.

His grandmother started the second portion of the enchantment, ready to siphon power from Audrey's family. He had no more time to lose. Israel tossed out the first spell he thought of, silencing Annabelle. His grandmother's eyes widened as her lips shut and sealed together. She ripped through the spell easily enough. She was in full power, after all. He prayed that whatever Audrey was doing behind him would work, but for now, he needed to stall before Kisasi's presence fully arrived through the gateway. He threw a spell at Annabelle that she deflected, tossing her magic back at him. Like a sickly slime, it slid off the shield he erected over him and Audrey.

No matter the magic he threw at Annabelle, even the magic that hit her and knocked her to her knees, she kept up the chanting. She was still strong as fuck, and that was partially his fault for feeding magic to their family. He cursed as a heavier flow of power was dragged from Audrey's family, surrounding the goddess's nearly firmed body. The women screamed out, and Annabelle laughed in satisfaction.

Audrey's voice was soft and firm behind him. Sharp shocks of electricity stung his back as she finally finished her spell. He didn't wait around for the result of it. Instead, he used his magic to send his sister's body back closer to the forest and out of the reach of his grandmother. The fire Annabelle had lit roiled higher, and a circle of light appeared. The gateway was wholly opened. Kisasi stepped from the flames, her slender body nude, her supple dark brown skin belying all the years she'd existed.

His hands froze midair as one of his grandmother's spells broke through their shield. He gritted his teeth, his bones aching and locking up as he fought through the magic. Audrey touched the small of his back, her power flowing through him and their bond. It steadied him and helped him break the hold over his limbs. Audrey threw a rune up into the space between her family and the goddess. It interrupted the flow of magic between the two.

Kisasi screamed in anger. "You would dare summon me and cheat me out of the sacrifice!"

Annabelle's eyes widened as she realized that Israel had only been stalling her so that his wife could do what she needed to do.

"No," Annabelle hissed.

"I will take my offering and then some!" Kisasi decreed.

Annabelle's body floated into the air as she screamed, a cord of power being pulled from her chest. Sabine was next.

"Power was given to your family and can easily be taken away."

Kisasi raised her hands, and Sabine's prone body was lifted, chest first, her head thrown back as his family's magic was stripped right before them.

The magic pulled at Israel, but Audrey's power bound him. It felt like his soul was rendering into two. Just as the pain got too much, the light of his wife's power wrapped around him. He closed his eyes as the goddess pulled against him, clashing against Audrey's magic. The energy seemed to double from Audrey. He managed to turn his head, and Audrey, Ness, and Nic were holding hands. Their family ties were easy to see. Instead of one cord of power, there were six, weaved tight, shining brightly as they held him to them.

Audrey gripped the back of his shirt as the goddess kept up her onslaught. His feet left the ground. There were several tense minutes where the night was only the goddess' indecipherable voice and the wind of magic. He didn't know what would happen to him or his family in the wake of the goddess' anger. Would she kill them all? Fear flared within him. It wasn't as if he wouldn't deserve whatever happened to him. For all the practitioners he'd sacrificed, for every shortcut he'd taken to power, Kisasi's punishment would be well-deserved.

His sister screamed his name, and Israel knew he couldn't leave her. He needed to fight the goddess's power. Not only just for Arianne, who would be left in the world alone but for the woman behind him, who was doing everything she knew to keep him grounded. Kisasi owned him and his family wholly, her power having sustained them for centuries. He wouldn't be able to break the goddess' ties on his own.

He'd hunted Audrey down, determined to force her to bond them, all so that he could use her power for his own selfishness...the irony that he had to use that same bond to give her his power to free himself from the consequences of his actions was not lost on him. Israel pushed as much of his magic towards Audrey as he could. Hopefully, it would feed her the extra energy she needed.

"No!" Arianne yelled again.

The fire around the goddess went out, and the wind picked up around his sister. She held her hand out towards the circle their grandmother had drawn for the invocation. The wind scattered the runes and interrupted the power. Arianne had come into her magic and used it to save them. Israel knew that the trauma from tonight would affect her and that magic, but he was thankful as the pain racking his body ended. The goddess' body flickered before disappearing. A hard whoosh sounded, and his grandmother and aunt's bodies dove toward the ground. Eli was there to catch Sabine, but not fast enough for his grandmother. Annabelle hit the ground with a sickening thud.

Israel didn't have far to fall, but the wind was knocked from him when he hit the ground.

Ness and Nic ran to their mothers while Audrey stooped down to him.

"Are you okay? How do you feel?" Her hands were shaking as she checked his body.

"You saved me," he whispered.

"You're mine. I'm not letting anyone take you from me," she said.

He pulled her to him, smashing their lips together. The love he felt for her overwhelmed Israel. He blinked away tears, unable to articulate the feelings that made his heart thud.

He pulled back as a thought occurred to him. "We need to do it now."

Do what?" Audrey asked.

He lifted the messenger bag from his shoulder. "Annabelle is at her weakest. We have to break the curse now if we're to make it work."

He pulled out the pages and handed Audrey the locket containing a hair lock he got from his ancestor's mausoleum.

"You're not in any state—"

Israel kissed her hard to stop her words. "We're doing this now. We may not get another chance."

"How can we help?" Kit asked, walking up.

The elegant gown she'd worn to the gala was dirty and torn in some places. The same could be said for all four women. He wasn't sure how Annabelle had managed to kidnap them, but they hadn't gone down without a fight. Kit's makeup was smeared on her face, but there was determination in her intense gaze. The reputation of the Fouche women was well earned. The strength they showed him humbled him.

Israel winced as Audrey helped him up. Damn it, she was right. He was exhausted. What the goddess hadn't taken, he'd sent to Audrey to help free him.

"I need power," he told his wife, almost reluctantly. After everything they'd been through, for him to turn around and do the thing he said he wouldn't...

"I trust you." There was no doubt on her face.

His heart clenched as their eyes met. She pulled his head down and kissed his forehead before pressing their heads together. He felt the heat and light of her magic as it entered his body, given freely along their bond. No ritual he could've performed would've given him this amount of raw power. He shuddered as she filled him. He didn't deserve her trust, and he certainly didn't deserve the faith she inundated him with.

"I'll show you everything you deserve. Until my last breath leaves my body, I'll show you how much you deserve love." She whispered in his mind.

"Enough, kitten," he whispered, choked up. Kissing her softly, he stopped her flow of magic. "We'll need to do this together since both families are at the root of it."

"We got this," she told him.

His aunt was groggy as she walked to him. "I don't...the goddess took almost all of it, but I will help with what I can."

Eli walked behind her, his sister clutched in his arms. "Sleeping."

He answered Israel's question reading his mind as always. He nodded and thanked God because he didn't want her to see what would happen next if his grandmother put up a fight.

He nodded and handed Sabine the pages as Audrey gave her Aunt Shelby the locket. He ordered Kit, Lauren, and Dawn to build another circle around his grandmother. Annabelle was waking as they worked.

"What are you doing?" She whispered, struggling to sit up.

"You're the family matriarch. You're tying this family to the curse." Israel told her absently as he worked on starting another fire.

"You..." Annabelle coughed. "I won't allow you to do this."

"You're in no position to do anything about it. How much power did the goddess leave you with?" He taunted as he drew new runes around the fire.

Audrey was chewing on her bottom lip as she used her magic to draw the spell components that she remembered from her session with Aunt Shelby. Whether or not they were in order or correct, she didn't know. But she traced out every rune and every subsection of the spell that had been weaved within her family. The magic floated over the fire contained by Israel's runes. Her family surrounded them, including the Taylors. She'd been relieved when they came from the front of the house relatively unscathed from their fight with the cat shifters. She prayed they suffered no serious injuries from it.

Her hands shook as she worked. She knew everyone, except maybe the shifters surrounding them could see the work they were doing. Doing magic in front of them made her nervous, and after everything they'd just been through, it seemed silly.

Shelby gasped as she finished. "Oh, Audrey," she whispered.

Audrey could hear the pride in her aunt's tone. She pushed her shoulders back, proud of how far she had come. Israel worked next to her, bringing up the spell from the pages of his grandfather's book as his aunt held them in place for him. He superimposed it over Audrey's spell, moving the parts around until they matched, laying directly one on top of the other. Audrey could see the details of the counter-spell as they tagged at the end of it.

"This is it, y'all," Audrey whispered as she lifted her hand to start the incantation.

"I want to keep my cat," Nic blurted out.

Audrey paused and dropped her hand. "Wait, what?

"Will breaking the curse take it from me? It's how I bond with my mate," Nic whispered. "I don't want to lose that."

Israel shared a look with Audrey, the flames dancing over his face in the darkening evening. Audrey turned back to the spell helplessly.

Israel squinted at the spell. "It's an all-or-nothing thing. If you keep the cat, all of you will have to live with it."

Unfortunately, she saw the same thing he did. "I can't...I don't know how to separate the spell in that way." Audrey whispered, feeling like she was disappointing them.

Nic gripped JT's hand, and Audrey felt the love between them. She turned to Ness in askance.

"I'm fine with it," Ness said quietly. "We're in this together."

They looked to their mothers. The sisters shared a look. Three out of the four older women had struggled for years with their cats. It wouldn't be fair to decide without their input.

"For my daughter," Lauren whispered.

Audrey knew how much it cost her aunt to make that decision. Despite all they had gone through over the years and the distance between them, her family still stuck together when it counted. She was so proud and happy to be a part of their family.

"Aunt Shelby," Israel said.

Shelby stepped forward and lifted the locket with their ancestors' hair in it. She whispered over it and kissed the metal before tossing it into the fire. The spell changed color, the fire rose high, and Israel and Audrey's hands moved in tandem, weaving the spell until it was spinning very fast. They released it, and it shot into the sky. The night quieted around them, and everyone looked at each other.

"How will we know?" Ness asked.

JT cursed as Nic shifted next to him. She jumped up her paws at his shoulders.

"There's my girl," he whispered, nuzzling against her head.

Tears clogged Audrey's throat. "It's not the full moon," she whispered. "I think...I...Aunt Shelby?"

Shelby also had tears running down her face. "There's only one way to know. If all of us can shift at will then..."

"But not out here. I want to do it in our safe space." Ness said.

Israel nodded. "Titi, will you take care of Annabelle?"

"Of course," she reassured him. "But, take your sister. I don't want her here for what comes after."

Audrey wondered what that meant but put it aside. She wanted a long hot shower and then her bed. She was burned out. Israel lifted his sister and whispered to her. He held out his hand, and Audrey gladly grabbed it. It was time to go home.

Chapter Twenty-Nine

Audrey wouldn't call the few hours of sleep she'd gotten restful, but they would get her through the day. There was still so much up in the air, and her curiosity wouldn't let her sleep in any longer. The sun was high in the sky, marking it close to noon. So...five hours. That was plenty. She rolled to her side and smiled at Israel's prone body. His arm was over his eyes, his usual sleeping pose. She would need to add blackout curtains to this room if he was going to stay. That thought sobered her a little. She still had a lot that she had to do here before she could, in good conscience, go back home with him.

She hoped he understood.

She braced her head on her hand and watched him sleep. She wanted to swallow him up. Love for him swelled her heart, and she couldn't help but crawl on top of him.

He grunted and slid his arms around her waist. "Nah, kitty cat, I'm sleepy as hell."

She laughed and nipped at his collarbone, licking against the bite to soothe it. Now that they'd broken the curse, she could feel her cat more. The animal was right on the surface, its instincts and extra senses at her fingertips. It would take a lot of getting used to. But, the need for touch, the whole body sensation the feel of Israel's touch gave her...top two perks, and it wasn't number two.

Israel said he was tired, and with their bond, she could feel the truth of that, but his dick was prodding her stomach in askance. Her body heated, and she rocked her hips against his. He groaned and lifted his hips but made no other move to satisfy the lust in her.

She snorted. "Fine. I'm getting up."

"Go," he grumbled. "We're safe here, for now."

She liked the sound of that. Kissing him, she crawled off him and headed to the bathroom to brush her teeth and wash her face. Her stomach was growling when she finished in the shower, and as she got dressed, she could smell the food cooking downstairs. For the first time since she'd left Israel, she was relaxed. There was no lingering worry about when he would find her and what he would do. But more importantly, there wasn't that crushing weight of what would happen if she tried to make their marriage work. It was a good feeling.

She smiled at Israel's sister as she rounded the corner to the kitchen. The young girl was sitting at the small kitchen table, playing on a tablet. Israel had spent most of the night with his sister in the guest room, ensuring she would sleep well in a strange place. Arianne looked no worse for wear, so that was a good sign.

Arianne looked up and gave her a hesitant smile.

"Did you sleep okay?" Audrey asked.

She nodded. "Lucky wasn't there when I woke up, so I came downstairs. Ness gave me this." She held up the tablet.

"Any good games on there?"

Arianne rolled her eyes. The expression reminded Audrey of herself at ten years old. "I had to get some because all she had was solitaire."

"It smells like Ness is cooking breakfast, so you're already off to a good start to the day," Audrey said.

Ness snorted. "I've already warned her about your cooking skills. Or lack thereof."

"Hey, I can make some stuff." Audrey protested.

"You're Lucky's wife, right?" Arianne's question caught her off guard.

They'd been introduced last night as they got her settled, but she couldn't remember if Israel had told her of their relationship status. Audrey nodded, interested to see where Arianne was going with her question.

"What do you think will happen now?"

"I suppose that's between you and your brother to talk about," Audrey said slowly.

"I would like to stay with Aunt Sabine. I mean, Lucky is great, but I just..."

"You don't have to explain. Savannah's your home. We would never rip you from your home." Audrey put a hand on her shoulder. "I'll talk to him for you."

Arianne nodded, and her face relaxed. The front door opened, and her aunt Dawn and Kit came in.

"I told y'all she would be cooking. Vanessa deals with her stress in the kitchen. Everyone wins." Dawn announced.

Ness sucked her teeth and slid what looked like a second pan of biscuits into the oven. There was another one cooling on the counter already. "Just for that, I ought to let you starve."

Dawn laughed and kissed her daughter's cheek. "I'll help."

The door opened again, and Nic and JT came in. Nic said a quick hello to everyone, looking around. "Where's mama?"

"Number five showed up this morning and told her she needed to get her fast ass back to the house." Kit answered.

Audrey covered her face, hiding her laughter. Dawn and Kit had no such compulsion.

"Well, she just might keep this one," Nic said with a smile on her face.

"Ness you baking?" JT asked.

She nodded.

"This the place to be then." He settled at the small table, careful to give Arianne space.

Isreal came down next and sighed. *"This too many people in the morning, kitten. If we're staying in Georgia, it's gotta be a little further away than your grandmother's house."*

Her heart stopped before thumping hard. *"You would stay for me?"*

"If you didn't learn last night, I would do anything for you." He told her. He leaned down and picked his sister up, sitting her on his lap. "Good morning, everyone." He said aloud.

"Will it be okay if I call TiTi?" Arianne asked.

He nodded and handed her his phone, moving the chair back so she could leave his lap. Arianne took the phone and left the room. Israel looked to Audrey.

"Did she say anything this morning?"

"She wants to stay with Sabine in Savannah," Audrey answered.

He sent a pensive look towards the hallway where he could see Arianne. Audrey didn't know how to decipher that look, but she and he needed to talk about their situation along with him and his sister.

"Talk later?"

He turned his gaze to her and nodded, kissing the top of her head.

"Mom, can I examine you for the curse later?" Audrey asked.

Kit gave her a surprised look. "Absolutely. I thought you would ask Shelby again."

"Just accept the peace offering, chile. Ol' passive-aggressive ass," Dawn fussed as she beat eggs across the kitchen.

"Not you in they business," Ness fussed as she sat down a plate of biscuits in the middle of the table. "That's why y'all can't get along for more than a day."

"They lasted a lot longer than I gave them credit for, if we're being honest," Nic said.

Dawn sucked her teeth. "Now see Nicole, I be sticking up for you, but now I see what my sister be talking about."

"What? I'm just saying."

"You always just saying," Kit jumped in, putting a biscuit into Nic's mouth. "Stay out of grown folks' business."

Israel and JT snickered, fixing themselves a plate.

Nic looked at Audrey for backup.

"Unh-unh, you see my ass be quiet when they fussing," Audrey said, getting up to get the jams.

She smiled as she helped Dawn and Ness set out the rest of breakfast. God, she loved her family.

Israel studied his wife as she nervously walked around her grandmother's workshop. The office was a small room, but the power imbued within was astonishing. Audrey finally settled, sitting crossed legs across from her mother. Both of them were within the confines of the circle Audrey had drawn. They'd both expended a lot of power last night, but that didn't seem to faze either of them. He knew he would need at least a day to recover. When they returned from Savannah, Israel had been shaken by the interaction with Kisasi. She'd stripped both his grandmother and aunt of their power, but when he'd examined himself, he'd found some of his power gone, but it was a negligible amount.

Had it been his bond with Audrey that saved him?

He was betting so. He remembered the first time he'd met JT in Miami when they'd done business together. The wolf's power had grown exponentially since that first meeting, all due to his mating with Nicole. It only stood to reason that the same would happen with him. Could the power Israel still possessed be power he gained from his wife and not lingering power from the goddess? It was hard to tell, and honestly, Israel had no plans of losing his wife, so he didn't care at this point. Besides, building power had never been a problem for him before. Thinking about how he could build on what Audrey already imbued him with had his fingers itching to get in his own workshop.

"I see keeping you on the straight and narrow will be my life's work."

Israel chuckled. Since their new bond, Audrey was a shadow in his mind. He would have to remember that in the future.

"Concentrate on your task. I'll behave for now." He told her.

She snorted and closed her eyes, breathing deep. When she opened them, he could feel the flare of her power. It pressed against the barrier of the circle, its strength shocking him once again. JT had been right. Patsy Fouche had not left her granddaughters lacking. He opened his inner vision and gazed at the magic she was working, startled by the complex spell. From what he could tell, she was reading her mother's aura but also moving deeper past that. It was intriguing. He pulled back and just watched Audrey's face. She tugged at her bottom lip with her teeth, the gesture endearing. The phone buzzing in his pocket pulled him from his thoughts. He looked down and frowned. Instead of disturbing Audrey, he walked outside to take the call. He looked up as Eli drove into the front yard. That meant Arianne had been home for at least an hour. He wondered why his aunt was calling.

"Yeah, Titi."

"She's gone."

Israel's stomach dropped, and for a moment, his world tilted. It wasn't grief that had him so off kilter. Annabelle had killed any potential for him to grieve her before he'd hit his teenage years. She'd treated Israel like shit...less than shit. He didn't care about her death. But her death marked a significant change in his life. He wouldn't have to look over his shoulder anymore...at least for her.

Eli walked up to him and raised his eyebrows. Israel waved him and his worry off.

"Are you okay?" He asked his aunt.

Instead of leaving, Eli sat on the top step of the porch. Israel joined him.

Sabine sighed. "I...honestly, Lucky. She was an evil woman, but she was my mama, so I'm conflicted."

Israel couldn't relate. But, he would always be there for his aunt and sister. The three of them were all that was left of the Deleon's.

"What do you want to do, TiTi?"

"With her gone, the territory will be up for grabs," she said. "I'm not strong enough, Lucky, and I gotta be honest. I don't want it."

That was a conundrum. With Annabelle gone, Savannah would be a power vacuum, and there was no telling who would fill it. Practitioners ran the gambit. The one who filled that power gap could be well-intentioned and powerful enough to keep out the vultures. Or... it could end up being someone just like his grandmother. That power gap needed to be filled before some other practitioner or rootworker stepped up and tried to take over. But, he liked his life in Miami. Plus, he needed to talk to his wife. He was no longer in the position to make decisions without her.

"It would keep us closer to my family, but not within popup distance."

Yeah, he would need to get used to her being in his head. She should've focused on her mother, but she was in his conversation way out on the porch.

She snorted. *"I'm wrapping up and will meet you in just a sec."*

"I'll need to talk to Audrey." He told his aunt.

Sabine let out a relieved breath. "Arianne would be happy having you in town with us. I know she asked to stay with me, but—"

"I'm not offended, Titi. I talked to her before she left. I understand. I'll talk to my wife and let you know what we decide."

"Thank you, Lucky. I love you."

"Love you more."

He hung up and sighed, turning to look at his best friend. "Thoughts?"

"Savannah's different than Miami. Bears out that way." Eli told him.

"You scared of bears?"

Eli chuckled. "Fuck you, Lucky. I ain't scared of shit." He sobered. "We ran from there the first chance we got. A lot of shit gone be stirred up when we show up."

"We're coming back a lot stronger than we left," Israel reminded him.

"Hell yeah," Eli muttered. "If the juice I feel is a fraction of what you got from Audrey, then we good on any block."

"So..."

"So, if kitty cat down, then I guess we can buss some heads. Start over and build some new shit."

Israel chuckled. "Hell yeah."

Chapter Thirty

Audrey leaned against the door frame of the front door and smiled at her husband and his best friend. In the four years they'd been married, she observed the closeness of the two of them. It was what initially had led her to give their marriage a try. She'd heard all manner of things about Israel when she'd first met him. After their drunken nuptials, she'd made it her business to learn all she could about her new husband. The information had been grim, and there had been moments when she'd been slightly afraid that she'd gotten into some deep shit.

But then, she'd observed him with his best friend.

There wasn't an evil bone in Elijah's body, and she'd looked. All the way down to his soul. Their friendship had lasted since they were kids. If her husband could sustain a relationship with someone like Eli and not corrupt him, then clearly, there had been something within Israel worth taking a second look at.

She hadn't expected that second look to turn into a third and then a fourth until she'd found herself tumbling in love with the asshole.

And God, did she love him.

"And what do you have to say about the matter, Wife?"

She sucked her teeth and closed the distance between them. Israel pulled her down into his lap, wrapping his arms around her waist.

"I gotta job now, and an hour commute is better than six."

He grunted at that.

"I'm not finna be chasing behind y'all keeping you out of trouble. I'ma tell you that right now," she warned them.

"That's your husband. I told you he stay wildin," Eli said, laughing.

Israel nuzzled into the crook of her neck, his nose cold from sitting outside. "What do you think, kitten? A chance to take over together, start some shit from the bottom up. You down to ride?"

She grabbed his beard, running her fingers through the coarse hair. "I like the sound of that."

She kissed him, and Israel angled his head to deepen the kiss.

"Alright now, cut all that out. Let's talk logistics," Eli grumbled.

"I have some stuff I need to take care of here with my family. Will the two of you be okay staying here for like a month or two?"

"I go where he goes," Eli gestured to Israel.

"I'll be wherever you need me to be, love," he told her.

Audrey nodded and took a deep breath. "Then, the two of us need to work on strengthening the wards around my family's property. There's a war coming, and I know how you two like to tussle."

As a person who worked hard to control their dreams, Israel was confused as he looked around the quiet, empty house. It was Audrey's grandmother's house. That much he was certain of, yet it looked so different than it did when he went to sleep. It stood to reason that it was an older version of the home.

Curious.

He'd never dreamed about the Fouche house prior to bonding with his wife. Was it a shared dream? He got his answer in the next second when Audrey rounded the corner.

"Lucky?" She frowned at him and walked over to him. "What are you doing here?"

"It's not me this time."

"I called you both," an older woman said.

She was a beautiful woman. Her brown skin had russet undertones, glowing and healthy. Her gray hair was braided in a single braid, draped over her shoulder. She wore a simple taupe linen jumpsuit that trailed her calves as she crossed her legs on the armchair where she was sitting.

"Grandmother." Audrey rushed over and gave the woman a hug.

This was the Fouche matriarch. Interesting indeed. Israel didn't move any closer to the woman, instead observing the loving look she gave her granddaughter. He was trying to puzzle how she was able to enter his dreams. She was not an ancestor of his.

Patsy chuckled. "Ah, but you're bonded to this family, now Israel Deleon."

"It's a pleasure to meet you," he said.

Her smile was achingly reminiscent of the woman kneeling at her side. She also had those dark cat-like eyes that he loved so much on his wife. The Fouche's were beautiful women, that was for sure.

"Now, I didn't call you both here for chit chat. I wanted to examine the bond for myself." Patsy stood and closed the distance between her and him. She walked around him and hummed. "Claimed him well, my darling."

Audrey looked sheepish. "Grandmother."

"It's good that you are bonded so tight. Israel will be able to do what you, my tenderhearted granddaughter, won't. You're well matched in that way. I like it." She patted his cheek.

He could feel her soft palm against his skin, even smell the perfume that she wore. Powerful, powerful stuff. "I'll do whatever I have to do to keep her safe."

"I believe that whole-heartedly. I thought perhaps the ancestors had chosen wrong for her, but seeing you and feeling your bond. I bow to their expertise. Don't fear the darkness you've cultivated within yourself, but don't let it rule you either, you hear?"

"Yes, ma'am."

He felt the love behind her advice. It was so different than what he received from his own grandmother. No wonder his wife grieved her so profoundly.

"I'll keep him from going too far," Audrey spoke up, moving next to him and gripping his hand.

Patsy chuckled, her amused eyes going between them both. "I don't doubt that. Between you and Elijah, I imagine y'all should be able to keep him on a wiggly line, if not straight."

He couldn't help the laugh that escaped. He could see where the women in their family got their cheek.

"Push her, Israel Deleon. Push her as hard you love her, and you'll come out of the other side of this with a love that will transcend even death."

He blinked back tears as feelings he couldn't even decipher rose within him. Her words touched a part of him that had been afraid that he wasn't fit for his wife. If he was getting the approval of this powerful woman that Audrey loved, then he must be doing something right. And he would continue to do that for as long as he had breath in his body.

Patsy cupped Audrey's cheek. "You got this, my love. Love him, teach him how to love you exactly the way you need, hear. Fouche's don't put up with no foolishness."

Audrey laughed, tears pouring down her face. "I promise."

Patsy nodded. "Then off with you two."

Israel sat up with a gasp, reaching out his hand until he touched Audrey's body. It was a dream. The most realistic one he'd ever experienced, and he'd spent plenty of time traipsing through his wife's dreams. He took a few deep breaths to calm his racing heart. When he got his breath under control, he turned to Audrey. She was on her side, her head on her palm, studying him.

"I love you," she said quietly.

He dragged her over onto his chest and devoured her mouth. He couldn't voice the strength of the feelings roiling through his body. He could only kiss her, using his tongue to hopefully convey it.

"I love you, Israel." She repeated telepathically.

He shuddered at her voice in his head. He would never get enough of that intimate touch. It was wild that she could walk through his thoughts and feelings unfettered. There was nothing he could hide from her, and while that would have scared him weeks ago, tonight, at this moment, he understood the trust and love that held their bond together.

He pulled back. "I love you is too tame for how I feel."

She straddled his lap and lifted her nightgown over her head. "You can show me."

He would absolutely do that...all night.

Epilogue

Vanessa Fouche was most at home in the kitchen. Her mother joked about it often and praised God for it twice as much. Baking and cooking always helped clear her mind. If life had been what she wanted, she'd have her own bakery, a loving husband at her side and a house identical to the one she was currently in. Her grandmother had done an amazing job with the renovations. It was almost as though the place had been made for Ness.

But. Life had never once gone her way, and today would be no different.

So, she tucked away her daydreams and pulled the pan of shortbread she'd baked for later out of the oven. Her family had already had breakfast and scattered to the winds once the kitchen was cleaned. Now, it was quiet in the kitchen, just how she liked it. Her phone buzzed in her back pocket for the tenth time, and she was finally irritated enough to answer it.

"Fouche," came the gruff voice. "You haven't been answering my calls."

Ness sighed and walked out to the backyard. "And yet, you didn't catch the hint."

"You can't hide in your little town forever."

"Just because you're scared to step foot on this land doesn't mean I'm hiding," she retorted.

"There's only so many chances I'm willing to give you."

"I'm done working for you. There's only so many more times *I'm* going to tell you that."

"We own you," he growled.

"So you think," she said.

"If I have to come there..."

"Promises, promises," she said and hung up.

She walked to the end of the back porch and sat down on the step. She smelled her visitor before she felt her. It was only like that with one person. Her grandmother sat down next to her.

"You still haven't told the girls that you see me," Patsy said.

Ness sighed. "Grandmother, you are but one in a line of spirits I see on any given day."

Patsy snorted. "You and that mouth. Audrey and her mate are going to strengthen the wards. But you're still worried."

Ness nodded and wiped a hand down her face. "The people that are coming, Grandmother, I worked for them. The magic wielder they have at their disposal...Yes, I'm worried."

"What does your deputy say?"

Ness sucked her teeth. "He's not mine."

"So you say," Patsy commented.

"Grandmother, you saw the way he straight up dismissed me. That man ain't checking for me."

Patsy chuckled. "Look at you pouting because your gorgeous looks aren't making it easy."

"I'm not pouting," she denied.

"I told Audrey to get ready for what was coming. Are you ready?"

Ness cursed. "How does one prepare to go to war with the government?"

"Not the whole government. Just a portion. That's easy work for a Fouche."

Ness snorted. This woman. Even in death, she had jokes. "Can I do this, Grandmother?"

"Chile, please, my blood runs through your veins. Of course, you can do this." Patsy reassured her.

"'It is not light that we need, but fire,'" Ness quoted.

"'It is not the gentle shower, but thunder. We need the storm, the whirlwind, and the earthquake.'" Her grandmother finished. "A fitting quote for what's coming."

"It will take all of us," Ness murmured to herself.

"And all of you have answered my call. Including your deputy."

Ness sighed. "I don't have time for love."

"Ah, but love finds a way, does it not?" Patsy said before disappearing.

"My ass," Ness muttered.

Though Patsy's words had hit their mark, Ness was equally adamant that she didn't have time for a relationship. Yes, the curse was broken, but she'd made a mess of her life. One she could only hope wouldn't drag her family down with her.

Also available from Dria Andersen

Chasing Savannah

The Knight Brothers

Hers to Call

To Her Rescue

Destiny Series

Georgia Arcana Series

A Destiny Awakened

Surrender to the Moonlight

A Destiny Revealed

Magic in the Moonlight

Escaping Destiny

Haven Series

The Hamilton Brothers

Haven

The Friend Contract

SoulBonded

The Alpha's Affair

Hellbound

About the Author

I am a full time photographer, and a mom of two. I've been writing my whole life, and after the birth of my first kid, I decided I couldn't very well bring up a fearless human without first trying the things that scared me. So, I wrote my first book, and then subsequently more.

I try to write stories I love to read: love stories that feature brown girls like me. Some of my stories feature gods and goddesses, and creatures I derived from old, African folk tales remixed and thrust into a modern world. Visit my website, www.driaandersen.com for more information on my other novels.

Join my newsletter!

www.ingramcontent.com/pod-product-compliance
Lightning Source LLC
Chambersburg PA
CBHW061201210726
48294CB00006B/1711